AN IDOL WITH LUV

PIPER J. DRAKE

ALSO BY PIPER J. DRAKE

Mythwoven series

Wings Once Cursed & Bound

Mystic Bookstore series

The Ink that Bleeds

Triton Experiment series

Hunting Kat, Tracking Kat, Fighting Kat

London Shifters series

Bite Me, Sing for the Dead, Survive to Dawn

True Heroes series

Extreme Honor, Ultimate Courage, Absolute Trust

Total Bravery, Fierce Justice, Forever Strong

Stand alone titles...

Siren's Calling; Red's Wolf; Finding His Mark; Gaming Grace;
Evie's Gift; Keeping Cadence

Want the earliest updates, sneak peeks, and exclusive content
from Piper? Sign up for her newsletter.

To Gail Carriger and Kelly Gallagher.

Thanks for all the music recs, video links, and playlists!
Beyond all that, thank you for the love and laughter.

CONTENT WARNINGS

Suspected murder, why choose, explicit consensual sex

THERE WERE a lot of ways Nirin could've recognized exactly what space station she had boarded, and hers was the corridors. Out of all the stations she had traveled to in the universe, only Daotiem Space Station had corridor floors set with tiles of sand and crustacean shells suspended in clear resin. The design was a nod to the planets that had funded the station, and a reminder.

Across known space and the various galaxies humans populated, there were other outposts and space stations equipped to sustain terrestrial and aquatic populations, but none of them were designed to ensure the two intertwined as much as Daotiem. It was a feat of architecture, honestly, and no matter how tired Nirin was, she couldn't help but smile at least faintly as she stepped onto the station and caught the subtle sparkle beneath her feet. This place was more than just five biomes attached to a central hub—three of them water habitats and two terrestrial—floating at the edge of a solar system located on the back end of civilized space. A location that most only ever passed through on the way to somewhere else. Daotiem was the place she always returned to.

It was also the place she consistently tried to leave as soon as reasonably possible.

It was late, based on station time. She briefly considered whether it was wiser to take a quick nap or stay awake and just power through the next station "day" to increase her chances of sleeping through the entire night. The latter was generally her go-to tactic for adjusting as quickly as possible to local time, wherever she found herself to be in the universe.

But she was also tired. Exhausted. The kind of fatigue that went past muddled thoughts, dry eyes, and itchy skin and into bone-deep aches all over the place. It was very possible for her to sleep more than a full cycle and just wake up incredibly hungry the day after tomorrow, station time. Come to think of it, she could hook into a saline drip to help her rehydrate while she slept. The thought was extremely attractive. But it was never a good idea to allow herself to wake up starving. It wasn't just about self-care. It was about public safety.

Fine. She'd pull the last bits of energy she had and get some sustenance from one of the food carts open around the clock in the core promenade, then head to her quarters. She punched the elevator button, then stiffened as she heard the barest whisper of sound in the service corridor to her right.

"Well, well, welcome back, stranger." A familiar voice broke the quiet around her.

She wanted to groan, but even the effort to dredge up that reaction was too much, so she settled for curling her lip to reveal her very strong, very sharp canines.

The owner of the voice stepped out of the shadows and leaned against the wall, muscled arms crossed over his broad chest. "Big teeth don't scare me away. Is that what happened to the rest of the crew?"

She shrugged. "Captain is still on board, if you want to have a word with her. The rest came ahead of me and scattered as soon as their boots hit station. They'll be all over the place by now."

"I came up to check on the docking mechanism and make sure everything was in order after you arrived." The corner of his mouth turned up, and a spark of challenge lit his gray-green eyes.

"Dietyr." His name had come out on a growl. It always did. Because he never failed to prick her temper within seconds of meeting up again. "It's been at least a decade—closer to two—since I wrecked a module during the docking process."

"But I was there and I remember." Dietyr's smile widened to a toothy grin.

Translation: it would take just as many decades or more before that memory went away.

Too late, she realized her mistake. She'd risen to his bait and now he was fully engaged. She sighed. She couldn't even claim exhaustion anymore, because the minute his scent had reached her—he always smelled of freshly laundered fabric and sun-dried grass, a scent uniquely his—her fatigue had melted away and her body had kicked into overdrive. Well, her body could wait until she took care of it herself, in the privacy of her bunk. All this newfound energy just meant she was definitely hitting the food carts on the promenade.

Without Dietyr. That was the important part.

"You can pretend you're not glad to see me, but at least part of you is." The line would've been creepy, but Dietyr's tone was quiet. Serious. Of course, his sense of smell was every bit as sharp as hers, and no shifter could miss the mutual arousal filling the hall. It always did when they were in the same place.

No hiding. No lies. Not about that.

He pushed away from the wall and stepped toward her, shaking off the relaxed attitude and walking with purpose. In contrast, his smile was still in place. His hands were open, held away from his body. See? Nothing threatening here.

That was some Gliesean bullshit.

"It's hard to deny yourself when your scent gives you away. I've respected what you've been saying the last couple of times you've been on station. But you're not happy, Nirin, and we both know it. It could be time to change up the pattern." His voice was all easygoing, almost gentle. As if attempting to apply the slightest pressure possible. "How about it? Stay at my place this time."

"Nah." Nirin kept her tone as equally light as his last statement. He'd been off to a good start, actually. She'd been leaning into his invitation until he'd gotten just a little too casual.

She started to walk away, but he planted his hand on the wall, his arm blocking her way. He'd given her room if she really wanted to leave. She could duck under or back away. But she'd only be going as far as the lift, which still hadn't arrived, and she wasn't in the mood to keep up the evasive maneuvers for long.

She studied the definition of his exposed forearm below the rolled-up sleeve of his station suit and then his bicep, which clearly stretched the fabric. He'd been keeping in top condition. He was always a beautiful example of the—mostly—human form. The problem with him was inside. He was broken.

So was she.

They were a bad combination, and she didn't need to repeat the same mistake.

"You take a lover in every port." His voice was low, husky, as he leaned into her space. There was no accusation, only curiosity, with an undercurrent of caution. "Why change your mode when you come here?"

"That's different." Because this was the closest place she had to home.

"Why not me?"

Anger was starting to simmer low in her belly. He knew why. "You don't want to have this conversation."

He tipped his head closer, enough that she'd have had to turn away to avoid eye contact. "I've been wondering for a while now. You always say you don't back away from any discussion, no matter how . . . complicated."

She barked out a laugh. It was the truth, so she would give him a truth in return. "You generally have prior plans."

It was tough to keep the words light. They were both trying so carefully to stop short of doing real damage with their words. She didn't want to imply any kind of accusation either. This wasn't about judgment over lifestyle choices. The both of them had made a lot of positive progress in learning to enjoy themselves and the company of others in healthy ways over the years. This was between them.

"I'd change plans for you."

She stared at him, letting her anger shimmer in the air between them. "Not nice to your on-station companions."

"Most of them wouldn't care. None of them care as much as you do." His gaze was steady, intent. "You can love men. You enjoy all different physicalities. I know you like my body type."

She let her gaze fall to take in the full length of him. He

was big and broad across the shoulders—and through the chest—tapering to a lean waist and hips. Built for a combination of power and speed, trained for optimal agility, he was a match for any merc she currently crewed with and most of the ones she'd met over the years. And his hands, ah, his hands. He had a strong grip on a weapon, and yet his fingertips could skim across a circuit board with the delicacy of a Lyraean dragonfly. Plus he knew how to use claws, when the situation called for it, both in battle and in bed.

Abort. This was not the time for reminiscing.

She lifted her gaze again, lingering on his lips for just a picosecond too long before looking into his eyes. It wouldn't take much at all to close the minimal distance between them. "It's not about body types."

His expression shifted slightly, losing some of the bravado and finally reflecting what had probably prompted this conversation in the first place. He leaned in even closer. "Then what do you find wrong with me?"

His lips brushed hers on his last word. The heat of that barest touch shot through her to every extremity, pulling at her. She forced herself to smile while keeping the tiniest of distance between them, her eyes open to continue looking into his. "We don't seek enjoyment for the same reasons."

Hell. She wasn't judging him for being with any number of people. She wasn't particularly different. It was why he chose the people he chose. And she didn't want to acknowledge she had anything to do with that personal driver.

She had breathing room, suddenly, but his arm was still blocking her path. He was silent for a moment, then he chuckled. "You've got too much patience. You'd stand here until I finally gave up on this conversation."

Yup.

"I usually do by now," he admitted ruefully. "But I'm not in the mood to give up without something new this time. I want to understand. Please, Nirin."

The sound of "please" on his lips undid her. Thankfully, he'd said it for a request for information. She breathed out, slow and even, bracing herself. "We choose our company for an hour, maybe a few, maybe a whole night. We enjoy. The experience doesn't change us. That's healthy."

"Yeah." His agreement was immediate. Of course it was.

"Why do you care that I never take you up on the offer?" she shot back at him, needing to force him into a little introspection too. "You said you'd even change plans for me. Why?"

He hesitated. Then he replied, "You aren't here that often. I could always catch up with them another time."

She gave in to just a little temptation and lifted her hand to his wrist, then traced the line of his musculature from wrist to forearm ever so lightly. Her gaze traveled up, across his shoulders, then over the hard planes of his chest. His skin was warm under her fingertips, inviting her to touch more. She forced herself to let go of the breath she'd been holding and withdraw, ignoring the lingering heat on her hands. This little bit was already achingly dangerous.

"Is that all? Just a question of availability? I'm a scarce commodity, so best to enjoy while I'm around?" She wanted more and hated herself for it. It wasn't fair to him. Not either of them.

She turned her head and pressed a kiss on the inside of his forearm, just where the artery ran under his skin.

He didn't answer her.

Of course not. Because the answer wasn't that simple.

Their scents were combining with a chemistry she wouldn't be able to resist much longer.

She met his gaze again and said the truth they'd both held deep inside too long. "We would change each other. Us. Together. Even just one more time would change us, and I'm not ready to try to walk forward after that."

No response, but the hallway wasn't silent. Their hearts were beating at accelerated rates, in sync. The both of them had the augmented hearing to know it too. They couldn't lie to each other. It was part of what, not just who, they were.

He straightened finally and let his arm drop to his side. She watched him for a beat, maybe two, then she forced her feet to move.

She'd made it a few steps away, into the lift, when he said the words to her back: "I am."

CHAPTER 2

JUN STEPPED out of the lift thinking maybe his manager was right: this station was so out of the way in relation to the more populated star systems, no one would expect to encounter him here. It might be exactly the kind of place he'd been yearning for, a place where he could disappear and blend in and focus.

Still, fans had popped up in the most unexpected places in every star system, every galaxy that he and the other members of his group had toured. He had absolutely nothing left to give his fans right now, so he wore a mask that covered the lower half of his face and a hood that hid the distinctive neon synth fibers threaded throughout his real hair. He would just pick up something to eat and take it back to the temporary quarters assigned to transitory visitors while his manager arranged for longer-term accommodations for him.

He was supposed to have stayed on the private transport ship Addis had chartered, but everyone on that spaceship had known who he was and tripped all over themselves interacting with him. He hadn't wanted to give them any bad experiences, but even the simplest interactions had been draining, them staring at him with idol-struck gazes full of expectations. If he'd remained on board any longer, he would have snapped at someone. Years of carefully nurturing his career, hard work, and branding would have disintegrated.

He couldn't. The other members of his group, his manager, and the staff who'd worked so hard to support them all deserved better.

So he'd disembarked before he'd made a mistake, and now he was hiding here on this small space station. Only, he couldn't just hide and starve. This core promenade was supposed to have food services around the clock, and no one would expect a popular idol singer to be right out in the open like this. It would be fine. No one even seemed to be looking his way.

The promenade was a reasonably large platform in the center of the station's five biospheres. He thought it was a pleasant-enough place . . . for the middle of a space station on the edge of nowhere. Five walkways—each originating from the connecting corridor of one of the biospheres—intersected at the center, and curving paths linked them at the outer edges. Raised planters held a variety of temperate-atmosphere broad-leaved plant life, which filtered out any hint of recycled air and kept the breathable atmosphere fresh. Food carts were scattered along every walkway, far enough apart that scents and lines wouldn't mix, but close enough for people to order from multiple carts and loop back to gather their orders.

It was the middle of the "night" according to station time, and there were very few people besides him. In fact, it seemed only a third of the food carts were serving freshly cooked food. The rest were unattended and had packaged meals ready to warm and consume, once a person with a station ID tapped to apply the price of the meal to their personal account.

He started toward the nearest cart with an actual person cooking when he saw a striking figure striding toward him. He froze, panicked. Had he been recognized?

The food cart vendor called to their neighbor, "Oi! She's back. She'll want the usual."

Ah. No. He was just in the line of sight of the person headed for food.

She, whoever she was, was curvy and compact, with pursed, full lips and a fierce, dark brown gaze locked on her intended destination. Her momentum carried her right past him, leaving his heart pounding. He sort of wondered if he'd had a close brush with something dangerous. Her hair had an asymmetrical cut, the tips brushing her angled jawline on one side and descending to her collarbone on the other. Her clothes looked comfortably worn in, made of some kind of canvas-like material—the kind that traveled well and didn't wrinkle. The fabric stretched as she moved, minimizing any constriction, and he thought he saw extra stitching reinforcing the major seams in her shirt and pants.

He looked for those kinds of things in his stage costumes when he was planning to go on tour. Luxury fabrics were for direct meet and greets, parties, and events. But when an idol was going to be wearing the same costumes night after night while moving through physically challenging choreography in various intergalactic concert venues, it was better for the costumes to actually be made to last.

Her clothes were coordinated shades of gray and blue; they'd probably blend into the background of any space station in any kind of lighting. He tended to choose costumes with bright or intense colors for the stage, but chose colors similar to hers to blend when he actually wanted to walk somewhere with a hope of going unnoticed.

Like now.

Which wouldn't work for much longer if he just stood there staring conspicuously.

He approached the food cart he'd originally been heading to, but stopped over an arm's length away to give the woman space to order. Wow, her presence was in no way less intense close-up. She projected "bother me and I can delete you" in her upright posture, arms crossed over her chest and weight balanced evenly over both legs, a little forward lean on the balls of her feet. She could have been a dancer, or maybe a fighter. She looked all solid mass, with her broad shoulders and upper body that tapered slightly at the waist and curved out to hips and strong thighs. He . . .

He should stop there.

He closed his eyes and shook his head. It was one thing to assess another being for their movement capabilities and the overall feel they projected. It was another to judge, positively or negatively. His industry was saturated in judgment, and the irrational appearance standards going in and out of fashion were never-ending cycles. He hated the way fans talked about his figure, his long legs, and his sculpted abs. Sure he was proud of his body and he liked to look fit. But he didn't like the way fans made assumptions about how he was managing his physicality, or argued about what he *should* look like, on the message boards and forums. He never thought he'd be drawn in by someone else's appearance the same way. People deserved better. So he'd stop there. Before he disrespected this person inside his own head.

"Got your tteokbokki, right here," the vendor said.

"We're just waiting on your ramyeon to finish and I'll mix them for you."

Apparently she was a regular, since the vendor knew what she wanted.

"No need." The woman's voice was unusual to Jun's trained ear. On the deeper side of mezzo-soprano, with a husky quality to it. "I can do it myself."

The vendor waved away her comment and gave her a kind smile. "Tastes better if we mix them here over heat. Less mess. This way, you can take it back to your quarters and focus on enjoying. You want fish cakes or fish balls for protein?"

Obviously, she was well liked. Definitely a regular.

"Fish balls," she responded. "And a soft-boiled egg on top, please."

Ramyeon and tteokbokki. Soft, bouncy noodles mixed with chewy rice cakes in spicy sauce. The protein choices sounded good too. His mouth was watering.

Jun cleared his throat and lifted his hand, one finger up. "I'd like the same."

The vendor looked at him in surprise for a beat before calling to their neighbor to prepare one more serving. Then they chuckled. "Not many ask for this, but whenever Nirin comes home, people remember how good it tastes and we get a bunch of orders."

Jun looked around. There still weren't many people around at this time. The woman, Nirin, snorted.

The vendor only laughed more. "Always, you order this. Always. Any time of day. It's a small station. People notice when there's an interesting twist on the usual. They want to try."

Well, it was good Jun had encountered her when there

weren't many people around. He didn't want to be anywhere near a thing people noticed.

The cook at the other food cart began jogging toward them, carrying two bags in one hand. "Here we go—oh!"

They tripped over the long hem of their apron and stumbled forward, then caught themselves but not the bags of ramyeon, which went flying. The vendor of the tteok-bokki cart jumped up and snagged one bag, but the other bag kept coming straight at Jun. Jun started to pull his hands out of his pockets to catch it, probably too slowly. He was going to end up with a face full of steaming-hot noodles.

A different hand shot out and seized the bag, right in front of his face. He stared at the hand, which was covered in an open-fingered glove, and blinked rapidly as it quickly disappeared from view. Nirin turned with the bag of noodles and placed it on the food cart.

"Th-thank you," he stammered, surprised and maybe a little embarrassed.

He thought of himself as someone with quick reflexes. Hers were far quicker.

She only grunted a response.

Unphased, the vendor began mixing the ramyeon, broth and all, with their tteokbokki, in the same bowl. "How long will you be on station this time?"

Nirin shrugged.

"Ah, well, stay for a little longer, why don't you? Seems you're away longer than you're ever here." They cut zucchini in half lengthwise and sliced it thin, then added it to the mixture. Then fish balls. A drizzle of what smelled like sesame oil followed.

Heaven.

Jun was glad for the high-end, two-way filtration on his face mask. It eliminated harmful particulates but still allowed for some scents to come through. He was betting the food would smell even better when he got back to his room and could take his mask off.

"I go where there's work for me," Nirin said.

It'd be interesting to know what kind of work she did. Dancers and other performers didn't usually live on out-of-the-way space stations like this where there weren't many jobs. She could be in entertainment, like Jun, but he doubted it.

She had a powerful but cold and prickly presence. Intimidating. Dangerous. Very much shouting "keep your distance." Whatever she did, it likely involved great reflexes and movement capabilities. There were a lot of professions in the universe for her.

He wasn't sure why there wouldn't be any work for her here, but then again, this was a small space station. He'd come here to hide, but he had no plans to stay forever. She could have her reasons for leaving too.

The vendor separated the food into two portions, then put each in a biodegradable box and added wobbly soft-boiled eggs. The woman, Nirin, bumped the ident reader with the back of her wrist, letting it beep verification of the charge to her account, then snagged her package and walked away.

Jun approached and did the same, glad his manager had given him a temporary ident with an alternate identity. "Thank you."

"Enjoy." The vendor smiled and nodded while wiping down their workspace.

By the time Jun picked up his own food and turned, Nirin was already completely gone from the promenade. It hadn't been more than a few seconds, and she'd already traversed the long walkways and vanished.

"Wow," Jun muttered under his breath.

It wasn't only her disappearing act. It was the entire encounter. He couldn't remember the last time anyone had made such a strong first impression on him, and he came in contact with countless people every day. All kinds of impressive personalities and beautiful faces, people of high status and influence. Maybe it was his burnout, but all those personalities had begun to blend together like white noise and static. But her face and voice stood out in his mind. She was just . . . impactful, in the best kind of way.

Even after he'd walked back to his temporary lodging and started to eat his food, he thought about her. Her taste was unusual, and he was glad he'd encountered her, because the texture combination of ramyeon and tteokbokki was fun. The savory, salty, slightly sweet sauce had a spiciness that built with every bite. The fish balls had a tender texture to them, lighter than red meat would've been but satisfying. He made a mental note to ask for this again in the future, even after he left the space station, and he wondered if he would meet her again.

He hoped so.

CHAPTER 3

THE SOUND of the incoming call was quiet and discreet, but Nirin growled as she rolled over to tap the vid screen. She'd intended to sleep until her body woke up naturally. Answering a call at . . . 0600 station time on the morning of her arrival was not the plan. The vid screen blanked, then projected a three-dimensional hologram of the caller. The head and shoulders of an old friend floated at the side of Nirin's bunk, at about eye level. She didn't even bother to sit up and pretend to be civil.

"What?" she snapped.

"How much sleep have you had?" The hologram of Addis Fionn grinned at her.

"Less than you," she snarled.

Wherever they were in the universe, they had already been up long enough to put together their look for their day. While they had left the beard growth around their chin and mouth at a sexy-stubble length, they had carefully cleaned up the edges of their beard so their high cheekbones could be defined with the perfect peach-gold bronzer. They'd gone for a bold combination of hot pink eyelids and deep royal purple shadow in the outer creases of their eyes, with bright teal highlighting their brow bones. White eyeliner sharpened the overall effect, and delicate pops of white shimmer on the inside corners accentuated the natural sparkle of mischief in their hazel eyes.

They fluttered long lashes with actual Albireon swan–feather extensions as they studied her hologram on their end of the call. "Darling, there are few beings in this world who can manage to look as sexy as you all rumpled from sleep and grumpy. If I thought you wouldn't hunt me down for doing it, I'd call to wake you up on purpose. Often."

How dare. Anger born of sheer indignation started to burn hot, then fizzled away as Addis winked at her and smiled wide enough to dimple. She sighed. "I probably would've woken up in the middle of the day anyway. Might as well get up now and make it through the day before trying for a full night's sleep again."

Nirin glanced at the computer terminal to confirm the hologram settings were set to project only her head and shoulders to Addis, then sat up and swung her feet over the side of the bed. She'd barely had enough energy to enjoy her ra-bokki last night, shower, and pull on a clean tank top and briefs before falling into her bunk. She wasn't going to bother with a bra or pants until she'd managed to get some caffeine into her system. As she stood up and took the few steps to the other side of her domicile, Addis' hologram followed her, maintaining a position at eye level so they could continue their conversation as if Addis had been in the room with her.

"We've established your waking me up was an accident this time and that you value your life, so you won't be trying to do it on purpose anytime soon." Nirin set the potable-water dispenser to her preferred temperature for brewing coffee, then turned away to give it time to heat. "Why did you call, Addis?"

"I've got a job for you, darling, and I'm calling in a favor."

Nirin turned to face the hologram and narrowed her eyes. "This is a first. You don't generally need my services."

Addis was in show business now. She and they went back a long way, at least three decades, probably four. Long enough for them to be very different people than they'd been back when Addis had helped her out of an impossible situation.

Actually, now Addis was the best talent manager across multiple galaxies and managed some of the most popular music groups in the universe. They were also one of the better souls Nirin knew. No one was purely good, really, but Addis was a person of solid integrity.

They truly cared about the creatively brilliant beings they managed. And they generally played fair when it came to building careers and manifesting opportunities for those they represented. So they had no need for a mercenary whose skill sets leaned violent when getting things done or eliminating potential problems.

"Ah, but some of the things that make you very good at what you do are your intelligence and adaptability." Addis lifted their chin. "I require unusually discreet security for one of my talents. Need a heavy hitter that doesn't look like security at first glance. Someone who can ensure my talent's safety and privacy while he takes some urgently necessary time off to rest and recover."

Nirin scowled. "You want me to babysit?" She placed a conical filter into a funnel, then ran potable water over the filter, wetting it edge to edge. She set it on a carafe to drain completely.

"Oh, if it were that simple." Addis laughed. "This talent has a truly rabid fandom. He's been stalked, hounded by press, and pursued by countless beings looking for everything from his money and fame to his love or even just his body. He's burned out. He needs downtime to get back his energy and his creativity. He needs to be where nobody wants anything from him."

Well, it was good this guy had Addis caring about him. She didn't know much about the entertainment world, but she got the impression it was as cutthroat and opportunistic as her own line of work in its own way.

"I feel for him," she admitted. She measured out coffee beans from a bag she'd brought on station with her. Then she poured the beans into a grinder and raised her voice to speak over the noise. "Do you really need me to watch over him at one of those luxury-resort planets? They've got their own security and they cater to the highest levels of society."

Addis shook their head. "Not the right kind of place. He won't be able to relax there, regardless of the luxury. Those places all know exactly who he is. It's their business to recognize him, do everything in their power to cater to his every whim, and oops, incidentally be recorded doing it so his armies of fans decide they want to enjoy exactly what he's enjoying. Suddenly, it's not a sanctuary anymore. Even the most discreet establishment can't plug up the info leaks when it comes to him. It's more effective to keep his security small, personal, and sourced from outside our industry."

Nirin raised her eyebrows. She hadn't thought about it from that angle, but she could believe that happened. No matter how advanced science and technology got in space, sentient beings—particularly humanoids—always found threats to make, vulnerabilities to exploit for a variety of reasons. All the high-end technology in those luxury resorts just posed even more opportunities for security breaches. And honestly, it was the nature of sentient beings to have differing priorities and ethics. The people component of any establishment was the weakest aspect of security design.

She lifted the filter and funnel, then dumped out the carafe and gave it a rinse with almost-boiling potable water before reassembling everything and adding the ground coffee beans to the filter. "So where are you sending this person and why do you think I'm the right kind of protection for him?"

"Last question first, I think." Addis tapped an exquisitely manicured nail etched in shades of indigo and magenta against the corner of their mouth. "At a glance, my grumpy fluffy puppy-bunny, no one would think of you as the kind of bodyguard we'd normally employ to protect talents in our line of business. We go big and ostentatious, so fans can see the bodyguards from across a venue flooded with beings. It's hard to even glimpse the talent when the bodyguard can completely hide them from line of sight. Besides, you clean up gorgeous when you decide the effort is worth it. You can pass as a companion or escort, if you decide the situation would be easier to handle that way."

Nirin chuckled. She placed the carafe and funnel with filter under the potable-water dispenser and set it to simulate pour-over pattern. Water at 90 degrees Celsius dripped in a circular pattern over the ground coffee. She paused the pour to let the grinds bloom. "It's been a while since I've needed to make use of those aspects of my skill sets."

"It'll be fun for you, then! Make sure to send me pictures." Addis fluttered their lashes again. "Your fighting skills are amazing, and if you encounter a situation no single humanoid operative can handle, you can always go all *rawr* on any attackers, in which case, you could take on a small army. I want vids of that too, if it happens. You fighting to protect one of my talents. The visuals! Oh my stars!"

Nirin held up a hand, palm side to their hologram. "I haven't agreed to this yet. Answer my other question."

She resumed pouring hot water over her coffee grinds, breathing deep and allowing the rich scent of brewing coffee to soothe her. This was her ritual at home and one of the major reasons she was listening somewhat calmly to Addis at all.

"You haven't said no yet, which means you're thinking about saying yes." Addis dropped their eyelids to half-mast and gave her a saucy smirk. "You don't even have to go anywhere unfamiliar. The best place for him is where no one would expect an intergalactic idol to be. I sent him to Daotiem Space Station. You just have to go home."

She glared at Addis' hologram. "Why here?"

"Oh good, you're already on station, so there won't even be any transit delay. Perfect." Addis clapped their hands in delight and started bouncing. Actual. Bouncing. "Daotiem is the perfect combination of out of the way, on the edge of nowhere, and a waypoint to everywhere else anyone wants to be. Very few permanent residents. But enough transient population to support a healthy economy, so the station has all the basic comforts. He doesn't need fancy, but he'll get the best rest if he can still be comfortable."

Nirin studied Addis for a long moment, long enough for their enthusiastic bouncing to slow and for them to start looking nervous. It wouldn't hurt to let them sweat as she thought things through. But really, she didn't have another job immediately lined up, and she liked variety in her work. She was probably going to regret this, but change would help fight off the exhaustion she'd been experiencing. No amount of sleep seemed likely to make it go away.

Finally, Nirin poured herself a cup of coffee, enjoying the rich scent of real roasted beans brewed the way she liked. This batch smelled slightly caramelized and had hints of milk chocolate and walnuts with sweeter notes of toffee. "How long? How much?"

Addis lit up with relief. "I'll pay you twice your normal fee, starting with five full day cycles. Could go longer, depending on how long he needs to recover from overextending himself. It could be weeks, could be months. I don't want to rush him, and he's worth the investment." They paused, their features softening into an uncharacteristically somber expression. "Help me give him the rest he needs, Nirin. He's a once-in-a-lifetime prodigy. The music he brings touches the hearts of countless beings across the universe. The way he dances is breathtaking. And his visuals! Really, it's important to help him get back to a place where he can create again."

Nirin wasn't sure she understood, but she believed Addis wouldn't put this much into a talent without reason.

"Did you arrange for accommodations?" There were actually a lot of choices on Daotiem Space Station. It wasn't as if she was going to hide this guy in her domicile. "My space is barely sufficient for me, and I choose a tiny living space because I'm hardly ever here."

"It's possible someone will trace it if I make any of the arrangements." Addis looked away from her, possibly at their data pad or some other computer-terminal surface. "I'll include funds so you can arrange what you feel is appropriate."

Nirin nodded, considering what else she might need to know for this. "I'll need his name and details on how I'm going to meet him and recognize him. His pronouns are "he" and "him," so I'm guessing he identifies as male. So there are spaces I'd likely not accompany him. Unless your company already has bodyguards doing that for your talents these days?"

"Mmm, true." Addis tapped a nail against the corner of their mouth again. "I'll trust you to decide whether you need any other resources to help you protect him. Cost isn't an issue here. I have faith in you not to take advantage of me."

Nirin ignored the waggle of eyebrows Addis gave her with their last sentence. "I'll need to let you go then. There's a limited number of beings I would trust on station and I need to move fast to get them before they take another job."

"Of course." Addis got instantly serious again. "Thanks, Nirin. We're good now. No favors left."

And their calling in the favor she owed was probably more valuable than the very substantial amount they'd just agreed to pay for this job.

She spent the next ten minutes reaching out to the rest of the mercenaries she'd just parted ways with last night. Every one of them either had another job lined up or had already left the station. "Oh, for the love of carbs and caffeine."

It figured. Mercenaries went from job to job, ship to ship, station to station. Sometimes they even went planet-side, though that was rarer: planets required additional specialization based on their environmental conditions and the nature of the job to be completed.

Sure, many lived the life for money. Some of them had a goal and got out when they made their fortune. But others, like Nirin, were in it for the experiences. Whether it was for the danger or excitement, or an outlet for anger or any number of high-energy emotions, they went from job to job, always moving. The minute they stood still for too long, they were dead, or stagnant, which was worse.

What she needed was someone as intelligent as she was, at least as strong, as fast or faster, and trustworthy. She needed someone who could take her in a fight or have her back in one.

She groaned.

Really, the only person she knew anywhere in this quadrant of the universe who fit that description lived here on station anyway. And he wasn't a mercenary. He was a station engineer.

If she wanted to do this job right—and she always made it her primary objective to do missions right—she needed to ask the one person she never wanted to work with again to join her on this job.

She poured herself a second cup of coffee and strongly considered adding a long pour of dark rum. Then she punched in the code to initiate a call to Dietyr.

CHAPTER 4

DIETYR FIGURED this initial meet and greet could go down in a few different ways. Glancing at the determined expression taking over Nirin's features, he decided it wise not to actually bet on any outcome as the most likely. In all the time he'd known Nirin—and it'd been a long time—nothing had ever worked out the way he thought it would when she was involved. Or the way she planned, either. For someone with such strategic and tactical strengths, she was the walking embodiment of chaos.

He grinned.

He loved that about her.

Nirin had contacted him a few hours ago about a job, with her, and told him the meet time and requirements. Bodyguard services for an intergalactic idol. Huh. He didn't have much other data yet, and he didn't care. It was a job. With her. On station. He had no idea if or when he'd ever have a chance like this again, and he was going to grab on to it with both hands—claws and teeth too, if necessary. Therianthropes like them were dangerously rare in the universe, but at least between the two of them, he and Nirin didn't have to hide what they were.

At the moment, Nirin was holding her hand open, palm side up, as she studied a holographic display suspended above her palm. She ended the projection by closing her fist, then strode down the white-walled corridor, which was accented with pink-and-green indirect lighting bordering signs to indicate private versus public areas.

This particular hotel was one of many similar facilities for travelers on Daotiem Space Station, and honestly, they were all relatively the same. All of them offered a place to rest, wash oneself, and address personal maintenance. Considering who they were looking for, he guessed this particular hotel had been chosen because it contained actual rooms with locking doors, as opposed to some of the ultra-efficient sleep pods and cubbies offered by other locations.

She paused in front of one of the doors, perfectly still.

Dietyr realized she was listening. He had given her at least a meter of space and wasn't going to hear everything she would, so he decided to move to the end of the hall, where he could keep watch for approaching people. As he took up a position out of line of sight but where he could still hear and smell anyone coming, she gave him a small nod of acknowledgement. He returned it. He'd been focused on engineering for the last several years, but that didn't mean he'd lost any of the skills he'd picked up in his days as a merc.

Nirin returned her attention to the door.

"Request access," she said quietly.

There was a long moment. She looked straight at the opaque door as if she could see through it. Dietyr opted to look up into the security sensor positioned closest to him in the corner of the hallway. Whoever was inside the room was likely using the basic displays. All hotel rooms on station had standard functionality for occupants to access security images just outside their door and in the hallway, as a way to determine who might be at their door before they opened it. Their client was likely trying to ascertain whether they were the kind of people he needed protection from or who would protect him.

The door opened, and Nirin gave a quick hand signal for Dietyr to join her. The two of them crowded into the tiny space, which had only a narrow walkway to the bed and then the wash facilities. There was literally just enough space for them to stand side by side with slightly scrunched shoulders. Their client had retreated onto the bed and was sitting as far back as he could manage, facing them, legs crossed in front of him. Curled up as he was, he seemed slight, with somewhat narrow shoulders. The look might have been purposely exaggerated, because he was wearing a ridiculously oversized hooded tunic. Though when the client's hands and wrists emerged from the folds of his sleeves, they were as small as Nirin's, slender, indicating a lighter bone structure.

"Addis said a contact of theirs was coming," the younger man stated, wariness still edging his voice despite having let them in.

His eyes were puffy and shadowed with lack of sleep. He swept one hand through his hair, the neon synth fibers in his blond hair glimmering amethyst, then teal as he did so. His rounded face gave him a youthful appearance, but those full lips . . . Damn, the man was kissable. No wonder he broke hearts around the universe.

Dietyr dragged his thoughts back to the job at hand. If Nirin caught even a whiff of his arousal around any client, she'd boot him off the job, even if it meant she had to work it alone. She could manage it solo, but she would exhaust herself doing so, and the shadows under her eyes were a match to their new client's. Both she and their client were in urgent need of a nap. Seriously.

And the image of the two of them curled up in the middle of the bed in front of him gut punched Dietyr like no other fantasy he'd ever had before. He mentally locked it up and tucked it away for safekeeping. He was going to want to revisit that later, and build on it in detail. Whew. Just not now.

"I'm Nirin, the private contractor Addis hired to provide you with personal security." She was wearing her professional expression, cool and calm, confidence inspiring. "This is Dietyr, the other half of your security detail."

Her mouth was set in a pleasant curve, and her lids were open slightly wider, so people could see their reflections in her eyes if they looked closely. People seemed to like that. Incidentally, she had her head tilted up enough for the light to catch her brown irises and give them an almost-golden, lit-from-within look. People responded to her better than they did to Dietyr, with his perpetually easygoing smile that rarely reached his eyes.

She wasn't much shorter than Dietyr, and while she had some lush curves, she was compact and traversed any space with light footsteps. No stomping around for her, unless she was doing it on purpose. His lower body was leaner, but he was even more muscular than her overall. People tended to identify him as the immediate threat simply because he carried more mass. Nirin had taken full advantage of that mistake in the past, often.

There seemed to be a persistent trait in humankind, no matter how far across the stars they traveled or how much they evolved: people always viewed the bigger predator as the more dangerous. As good as he had been as a mercenary once upon a time, and as sought after as a contract hitter, he was not the better killer between the two of them.

He dragged his attention back to the current situation and gave himself a mental shake. He was here because Nirin trusted him to do this job well. It was a chance. He didn't want to muck it up. There would be time later for him to process all the feelings churned up from being near her, on the job with her again. For now, he simply gave the client a nod and waited.

The younger man looked from one to the other of them. "Just call me Jun."

There was another pause, then Nirin relaxed her stiff posture minutely and it was suddenly a few degrees warmer than professional courtesy in the space between them all. "I hear you need rest and relaxation. I'm not sure if you've had a chance to learn about Daotiem Space Station, but if you can give me more of an idea of what you're hoping for, we can do our best to make arrangements to facilitate your needs."

Rest made sense. A tension eased inside Dietyr too. He was always wrestling with the desire to care for Nirin, pamper her. She had a thing against accepting help though. She would never let him nudge her into taking things easy. He did his best to respect her ability to take care of herself, but if this job was about ensuring the client got enough downtime, hopefully she'd have the opportunity to rest too.

He could do his part. Give her enough time to get her own rest in. She'd been taking job after job off station for too long, driven like she was being hunted herself. When he'd seen the state she'd been in last night on her return, he'd almost lost it.

Jun nodded, not quite relaxing, and maybe wary in response to the warming of Nirin's tone. "I need privacy, first and foremost. I just want a real chance to decompress and be alone. Interacting with anyone, even this, takes up way more energy than it should and I can't sustain it. I don't want to be a stellar asshole, but I will be. I can't not snap at people anymore."

She nodded and so did Dietyr. So far, it would be fairly simple to give Jun what he wanted.

"I'd like an environment that is peaceful, but ever-changing." He paused and took a measured breath. When they didn't say anything, only listened, the corners of his mouth lifted a fraction and he let more spill free. "I'd like things to do where I won't have to worry about being mobbed by screaming fans. I want to eat and enjoy simple pleasures and find my way back to the kind of happiness I tap into when I'm songwriting. All my songs lately have been angry and moody and brittle and I don't want that for the rest of my idol career. It's time for a change of pace and I can't seem to find my way back to more positive emotions. It's like I can't reach them, like they're gone . . ." Jun trailed off and blinked, then shot them a nervous glance as he gave what sounded like an embarrassed chuckle and rubbed the side of his nose. "So yeah, that's what I'm looking for."

He hesitated, then looked up at Nirin through long lashes. "The noodle-and-rice-cake dish you ordered last night. It was good."

What? Dietyr looked from Jun to Nirin. She hadn't gone straight to her bunk last night? She hadn't mentioned knowing the client. So it couldn't have been more than a passing interaction.

"You shouldn't go to the core promenade alone anymore," Nirin said quietly. She didn't sound surprised at all that Jun had brought up encountering her already. Only addressed it. There was no admonition or judgment in her tone, at least the way Dietyr heard it. She was stating a fact because it was her job. "To be honest, you got lucky last evening. I've never seen it so empty."

Jun stiffened for a second, then he nodded. Dietyr cringed though. Hard to say how their new client perceived her statement since Jun didn't know her as well. He decided to give Jun a grin and hope the guy took it as encouraging.

Nirin's pleasant, all-business expression held steady as she continued to focus on logistics. "Addis sent me the usual files and media kit, including your food preferences. No allergies to speak of. It'd be easier if you let one of us acquire and bring you meals, but if you like going out for your own meals, at least one of us should always be with you. Anything else we should know? We're to do our best to fulfill any reasonable request."

Jun stared at her, and a soft flush spread over his cheeks, then he shook his head. "The usual data files distributed by our agency are designed to reduce the chances of anyone taking advantage of our preferences. Anything listed as a favorite and gifted to me, I actually don't ever eat. Instead I'd appreciate exploring what food is good here on station. Anything outside my usual on tour would be a great change up. And I'd like for us all to speak casually to each other, if that's agreeable to you. I'm more interested in having experiences in friendly company when I'm not alone."

Jun was attracted to Nirin, Dietyr realized, and not just in a passing way. Jun was very interested in her. Hard to tell age in anyone these days with the way medical science had become more accessible to even the outer systems in recent cycles. Jun probably wasn't older than either Nirin or Dietyr himself, but anything between three and six decades was entirely possible and Jun's pheromones had the almost-musky quality to them that signaled an adult in his prime.

Dietyr might get ferociously jealous in some situations, but this wasn't one of them. After all, it wasn't like Jun was being obvious or aggressive about it. Unless his manager, Addis, had told Jun much about Nirin, Jun had no idea she could scent his desire, hear his accelerated heartbeat. To any normal human, Jun was outwardly polite and showing no sure sign of his interest.

Nirin had left herself open with her offer to fulfill any reasonable request. Dietyr decided Jun was at least a *mostly* good person for not having twisted her statement and tried to take advantage of it, or her.

"Well, first thing's first." Nirin looked around them. "This isn't bad for one person, but we're changing location to something that can fit all three of us."

Dietyr snorted. She glanced at him, narrowed her eyes, and added, "Comfortably, with privacy."

He grinned. It was just as well Jun was a reasonably good person, because Dietyr himself was a bit of a bastard. Innuendo was too much fun. Nirin's cheeks colored a peachy rose as she seemed to realize her addendum hadn't mitigated the possible interpretations. Jun covered his own mouth with a fist, and Dietyr traded amused glances with him. He was going to like Jun. And if anything, he had a feeling Jun wasn't going to take issue with Dietyr teasing Nirin.

"Right." Dietyr nodded to her and tossed a wink Jun's way. "More bed space, some room to move around. Copy that."

It was going to be a fun job, even if Nirin might kill him along the way.

CHAPTER 5

"SO WHERE ARE WE GOING NOW?" Jun asked.

He let his head fall back until it rested against the wall behind him. Somehow, the tension he'd been carrying through his neck, shoulders, and even his back was easing up for the first time in longer than he could remember. It had been there continuously, a constant reminder of all the things he had to do for his career and his bandmates. For his fans. Something about Nirin and Dietyr and their back-and-forth banter put him at ease.

"I've got a couple of options in mind," Nirin said.

Dietyr chuckled. "Of course you do."

Nirin shot Dietyr a frigid look, and Jun wondered how the man's heart hadn't stopped beating right then and there. But the big man only winked at Jun again—be still his own skipping heart—and sat on the edge of the bed, bringing Dietyr palpably nearer to Jun. Between Dietyr and Nirin, there was a whole lot of presence filling a very tiny space, and him thinking that said a lot, since he was accustomed to interacting with some of the most charismatic people across multiple galaxies.

"Okay, how many potential plans have you already prepared?" Dietyr asked, his back straight and broad shoulders relaxed, one ankle crossed over the other knee. "Hit us with your top three. We can consider the other dozen or so to be backup plans, right?"

Nirin glared at Dietyr, and Jun thought she might actually reach out and strangle him, or otherwise incapacitate him with some sort of efficient physical strike. Hurriedly, Jun leaned forward and spoke. "Please. Sit down too. It'll be more comfortable for us all to talk."

Nirin's attention was suddenly on him, and he was caught in the intensity of her gaze. There was a hint of a twinkle in her eyes, though, and he thought he caught a quirk of the corner of her mouth. Then she blinked and he could breathe again. She was fierce but not frightening.

She sighed. "Dietyr's not wrong. I did plan for multiple contingencies."

She perched on the edge of the bed, managing not to touch Dietyr somehow despite the two of them almost sitting knee to knee in the limited space. She extended her hand into the space between the three of them, her palm facing the ceiling, and initiated a holographic display. Three spheres formed, each depicting different images. One displayed leafy trees and a grassy, flower-filled meadow with fluttering butterflies. Another displayed deep forest and water rushing into a large lake. The third displayed an expanse of cerulean sea, with schools of fish flashing silver, gold, and green.

"Which of these gives you the most peace to look at?" Her question was delivered softly, with a gentleness Jun hadn't anticipated given her sharp edge conversing with Dietyr. Her calm tone washed over him, and tears welled up in his eyes before he realized what was happening.

Ah. Burnout did things to him; every one of his defenses really was worn thin. Damn it.

Jun cleared his throat and blinked back the wave of emotion. "The ocean."

The thought of floating weightless was amazing. Besides, he never had time in his tight schedules to explore waterworlds when they were on tour. It was easier to arrange at least a brief walk through nature in terrestrial venues because he was, for all intents and purposes, a creature of land.

Nirin only nodded and closed her fist on the holographs. "Then I have a resort in mind. I'll finalize the arrangements while you pack."

"Wait." Jun swallowed hard as her gaze locked onto him again. Dietyr was looking at him too, and having the both of them focused on him was all sorts of disconcerting. "I'm here to rest, recover from being overworked, but I also need to replenish creativity."

They knew that. He'd said that already, hadn't he? He clenched his jaw and forced himself to breathe as he wrestled the right words out of his brain to communicate what he wanted, not what he thought people needed to hear from him. This wasn't the time for him to be the people pleaser.

He cleared his throat and continued: "I can't do that pent up inside of a single hotel suite, no matter what kind of scenery it has. I'm an active person. I'd really like to do things too."

Nirin lifted an eyebrow and Dietyr grinned.

Jun couldn't help it; he grinned back. "All kinds of things."

There, let them both chew on that. He was burned out, but he wasn't an invalid and he wasn't precious or fragile. He was an intergalactic idol, one of the best in his professional field, and he was particularly known for his sex appeal. These two new bodyguards were not going to tuck him away into a hotel suite all meek and quiet like some child in time-out.

"Your safety"—Nirin's tone had turned dour—"is our primary objective." She scowled.

Dietyr, on the other hand, rubbed his jaw thoughtfully. "If anyone knows where there's things to do on this station, it's me."

"Every idea you have in your mind at this moment is likely to get Jun into trouble," Nirin retorted.

Jun decided he was getting in on this fun. He wasn't one to sit on the side and watch. Ever. The last vestiges of intimidation melted away as he sat forward. "Trouble can be fun and fun *can* be a huge factor in my recovery. Isn't even one of you more than qualified to keep me safe from anything we're likely to encounter on station?"

He raised his eyebrows at them and tilted his head to the side just enough for a few strands of his hair to fall across his forehead. It was only a space station, after all, and not even a large one compared to some he'd visited.

"I'd trust Dietyr with my life, don't doubt that," Nirin said. Something that might have been surprise passed across Dietyr's face and then was gone again. Jun noticed, but Nirin didn't seem to as she continued: "But anything he's likely to get you into would have too many potential threats for just one bodyguard to keep track of."

"Which is why you'll be with us too, right?" Jun rested his elbows on his knees, fully engaged now. He gave her his most charming smile.

Her eyes narrowed warily. "I'd intended for Dietyr and I to take shifts on watch. It's never optimal for a single bodyguard to provide round-the-clock protection for an unspecified amount of time."

Jun nodded, relieved Addis hadn't specified any kind of time limit. "But we could find a happy compromise in scheduling some adventurous excursions with plenty of rest time in between, right?"

Dietyr didn't say anything more, though he could have. He seemed in complete support, based on his wide grin and the laughter in his eyes. But maybe Dietyr was willing to tease Nirin, not undermine her. It was probably a very fine line. Jun's respect for the other man rose even further. Still, it was important to Jun to do more than sit inside a hotel room.

After a long moment, Nirin nodded. "Yes, we can figure out a balance between security and recreational activity. We can talk about specific options once we get you to a more secure location."

Dietyr held out a fist, and Jun bumped it with his own.

Nirin stood. "Pack, please."

"My carisak is right here and I just have a toiletry kit in the wash facility." Jun rose to his knees on the bed and reached into the overhead storage unit to retrieve his travel bag.

Nirin moved to the standing space by the door, just next to Dietyr, so Jun could comfortably get off the bed and access the wash facility. He quickly popped in and got his toiletry kit, then shoved it into his carisak. "Ready."

"From here on out, do your best to stay between the two of us unless one of us tells you different," Nirin said, turning toward the door.

Dietyr jerked his head, indicating Jun should follow Nirin. "I'll be right behind you."

Nirin was tapping the touch screen embedded in the

door, bringing up views of the area directly in front of the doorway and the immediate hallway. "Clear."

She palmed the door open and stepped wide as she exited, peering around the corner. Jun followed her. Dietyr was a comfortable breath or two behind him. They headed down the corridor and turned. As the next hallway opened into the reception space, Nirin held up her arm, her hand in a fist, and stopped short. Jun managed to halt before he walked right into her back. He peered around Nirin, not too hard a feat as he realized she was slightly shorter than him. She had such a strong intimidation factor, he hadn't noticed until he was up close.

There were police scattered around the reception area, and in the middle of the floor was a dead body.

Dietyr murmured, "I really want to know if she has a contingency plan for this."

CHAPTER 6

NIRIN TOOK IN THE CORPSE, the area immediately around it, and the various personnel around the room. Whoever was in charge had chosen to close off the reception area at the main entryway. There were no boundaries by the corridors leading to guest rooms, presumably because the only way out was through here. All the hallways for this transient hotel led back to the reception area. Anyone leaving the hotel was going to have to stop and likely be questioned.

A being moved away from the main group of police officers. She balanced on four tentacles that provided mobility the same way legs would for quadrupeds and headed straight for Nirin. Nirin waited, lowering her arm and motioning for Jun to remain behind her. Dietyr would keep Jun from stepping forward while Nirin did the talking.

She nodded to the approaching officer. "Officer Nyala."

Officer Nyala's hinged lower jaw dropped open in her version of a smile, revealing multiple sets of long, needle-like fangs. "It's been a while since you've been on station, Nirin."

Nirin lifted a shoulder in a shrug. "Not so long. I just don't generally stay on station for more than two full cycles."

"Last I heard, you still maintained a permanent residence on station. What brings you to a transient hotel?" Officer Nyala loomed over Nirin, even though she could have positioned herself on her tentacles to meet Nirin eye to eye.

The action was meant to present Nirin with a very good look into Nyala's jaws. Officer Nyala's main body was small relative to her (very dangerous) mouth and protected by a carapace across her back. Honestly, her jaws might have been as much as a quarter of her central body mass that balanced over her four tentacles. Intimidation was her main advantage when interacting with potential suspects.

Nirin didn't respond well to intimidation tactics. She stepped forward, almost under the police officer, so Nyala was forced to look straight down or step back to avoid giving Nirin unsupervised access to her vulnerable underside. Nyala opted to lean back on her tentacles without giving any ground. The position put the officer off-balance if it came to a fight. But they were both posturing at the moment. An actual fight wasn't likely to be necessary.

Which was a shame, because Nirin had often wondered which of them would come out the winner. They'd never had the opportunity to spar, and while Nirin had fought cephalopods in the past, none of those were specifically of Nyala's species. Strictly speaking, Nirin wasn't well suited for countering species that evolved in aqueous environs. Therein lay the appeal. She loved a challenge.

But now wasn't the time. Instead, she gave Officer Nyala the pertinent information. "Personal security contract. I came to pick up my client. You'll see two of us arrive on the hotel security feeds. The reception area was empty. Nothing seemed out of the ordinary. We headed straight to our client's room and remained inside until all three of us came out and made our way straight here."

Officer Nyala studied Nirin for a long moment, then waved a shorter arm lined with suckers. "That confirms what we've already seen from the security feeds. I'd like to ask your client some questions."

Nirin glanced at the main entrance. There was no press yet, but there would be some representatives arriving any moment. News was news, and a dead body would be a guaranteed headline on a station like Daotiem. "My client requires personal security and as much discretion as possible. If you don't have a very good reason to detain him, would you be amenable to meeting us in a better place?"

"You're moving him to a more secure accommodation?"

If Officer Nyala really wanted to take Jun back to police headquarters for formal questioning, she would have attempted an arrest already. Instead, she was respecting Nirin's stated position as personal security and going through Nirin. They had no reason to suspect Jun. They just needed whatever information he had. And Officer Nyala was good enough at her job to know a person provided more information when they felt reasonably safe and comfortable. Nirin nodded.

"Where?"

Nirin shook her head and held up her hand, palm open to indicate peace. "You are discreet. But no department on station, not even the police, is leakproof when it comes to the press. Even if someone doesn't give up information on purpose, anyone can be hacked. Better you don't know. We can meet tomorrow morning at Sunshine Bois. I'll ask Garek and Grigg to delay opening a bit so we can all sit down and have an informal chat over spritzers. Does that suit?"

Officer Nyala chuckled. "Good enough. I could use more people like you on my team. I've been saying for years that you'd make a good detective. You always anticipate the information we need and make sure we have it with the least amount of friction."

Nirin grinned. "The sooner I give you what you need to know, the sooner I can go about my business."

"I don't look forward to a day when you end up on the wrong side of the law."

Nirin kept her smile in place and didn't say a word in response. They both knew her occupation as a mercenary meant she existed in a gray area when it came to the law. Nirin had always been careful to keep her activities at least plausibly legal as much as possible, and if she had to blur the lines, she made sure she was never caught. So far, she'd never had to blur lines on Daotiem Space Station.

Officer Nyala sighed, the sound coming across as more of a bubbling hiss. "I have enough today in processing this scene and interviewing the handful of beings staying here. I can meet you and your client tomorrow morning, if you're giving your word. If I have any questions for Dietyr, I'll ask them then too."

While Daotiem Space Station was a waypoint along quite a few travel routes, there were lulls in through traffic. Nirin had studied the publicly posted arrivals-and-departures schedule for the station. There were only a few travelers staying between ship transfers now, and they had their choice of a dozen hotels like this one. That meant the chances of this one being even half-full were low. But Officer Nyala was thorough, and she only had two or three other officers here at the scene with her.

Nirin had gambled on Officer Nyala's willingness to follow up later.

Still, this had been somewhat easier than anticipated.

Officer Nyala moved to one side, indicating with one of her shorter sucker-lined arms again, this time for them to proceed along the wall toward the main entrance. Nirin made eye contact with Dietyr and tipped her head slightly to the side. He nodded in return and took the lead, tapping Jun on the shoulder so the young man would follow.

As Nirin moved to bring up the rear, Officer Nyala extended her arm to block Nirin's way. "You are very detail oriented and you do have the experience and skill sets to offer useful insight. If I need to bring you in to meet with our forensics team or other parts of the investigation, I hope you'll consider giving us some of your time."

Ah, there was the catch. Sure, Officer Nyala didn't have a particular reason to detain Jun. The officer could hold Jun for questioning, though—long enough for the press to get a look at him and any other suspects. For any normal being, that could mean a lot of uncomfortable news exposure, but for Jun, being involved in a scandal with a dead body could escalate into a career-ending experience. If Nirin wanted to minimize Jun's exposure, which was a part of her job, she would need to play nice with Officer Nyala.

"How long have you been waiting for this kind of opportunity?" Nirin gave Officer Nyala a sideways glance, then watched Dietyr continue with Jun safely out the main entrance.

"A while." Officer Nyala chuckled, unrepentant. "The mercenary life is a short one. Retiring is one of the better outcomes, and I know I'm not the only being who'd like it if you settled back here on Daotiem."

Uh-huh. Nirin wasn't going to entertain that discussion

either. Officer Nyala hadn't given Dietyr any kind of grief at all. That was going to be a private discussion between Nirin and Dietyr for sure.

"As long as it doesn't interfere with my current contract, I'll consider consulting for the police on this one case," Nirin allowed, finally. "For a fee."

"Of course." Officer Nyala backed away so Nirin had a clear path to the main entrance. "I'll have a contract prepared and sent to your personal dataspace."

"Fine." Nirin took in a long, slow breath. Then she moved to catch up with Dietyr and Jun.

This job was getting more and more complicated. A growl rumbled up from her chest, and she caught herself before it became audible. She wondered why she was so irritated by the delay. The corpse should've at least piqued some kind of professional curiosity in her. The chance to earn a little extra income should've made her happy too. So why was she in such a rush to catch up to her two guys?

Her partner and her client. Not her guys.

Tension wound tighter and tighter in her chest and abdomen and didn't ease until she joined them and they headed toward one of the main transportation tubes that would carry them elsewhere on station.

Together.

CHAPTER 7

JUN STEPPED out of the air lock and into the entryway of the suite Nirin had reserved for them, and he had to admit, the accommodations were way different from the places he and his band members usually stayed. When they were on tour, the staff chose hotels for their proximity and ease of transport to the concert venue, with security taken into consideration. This place wasn't near any performance venue and wasn't easy for terrestrial beings to get to, regardless of its proximity to other places in Daotiem. He'd never stayed in a completely underwater hotel before. Once or twice, he'd stayed seaside on a planet with his band members. But never quite like this.

"It's okay to make yourself comfortable," Dietyr said as he took Jun's carisak and walked into one of the bedrooms before returning to the entryway. Dietyr had been the first to enter, while Nirin had held Jun back, waiting for Dietyr to confirm the suite was clear. Whatever that meant. "Nirin will be in when she's done engaging the bubble barrier."

"Bubble barrier?" Jun asked, feeling off-balance.

Neither Dietyr nor Nirin had talked about the crime scene since they'd left the transient hostel. There had been a dead body, and they both were carrying on as if it hadn't even happened.

Dietyr jerked his head toward the living area, which had floor-to-ceiling windows surrounding a large, sleek couch and two armchairs. There was a gorgeous view of the oceanic biosphere: too many brightly colored fish to count swam around in coral-colony pods suspended a hundred meters above them by massive plasteel cords anchored to opposite ends of the space. Their suite was deep, relative to this biosphere's gravity, so there was less light and the waters directly around them were the hazy blue of oceanic twilight. At this depth, there were pods filled with air, attached to the same plasteel cords at intervals. Jun had asked about these pods as they'd passed them in the compact submersible Nirin had piloted to get them here. The air pods were for beings who might need air as they traversed the waters of the biosphere—the biosphere was designed to accommodate a variety of marine-based life-forms.

As he and Dietyr moved to a window, a multilayered curtain of bubbles rose from below, floated up, and surrounded the suite.

A moment later, Nirin entered through the air lock. "How are we settling in?"

"Still checking things out," Dietyr responded, his tone genial and upbeat.

"The bubbles are interesting." Jun found them mesmerizing, really. "Wouldn't the view be better without them, though?"

"Maybe." Nirin joined him at the window. "But whatever you can see, could potentially look in and see you. The bubble curtain is mostly for privacy. It also acts as a sound buffer. Many of the residents communicate through underwater sound and it can get chatty if they venture close to the suites."

"Ah." Yeah, Jun had no desire to be entertainment for any curious residents in any of the biospheres on station. "It's good to know I won't be accidentally peeking in on anyone who lives here either."

Nirin gave him a smile, and in that one beat, she morphed from severe and all-business to friendly and approachable again. She then stepped away just as quickly, leaving Jun shaken. He gripped his shirt over his sternum, considering the zing he'd experienced right to the center of his chest. It probably wasn't good for his heart, but it'd been fun, like an adrenaline rush, and he wanted to experience it again.

Which meant he'd need to figure out how to get her to smile at him again.

It couldn't be that hard, right?

Jun realized Dietyr was still standing nearby, at the window too. The other man's expression was thoughtful as their gazes met, and Jun briefly wondered if there was going to be friction. It'd be bad if one of his bodyguards developed a personal problem with him.

Instead, Dietyr only grinned and raised an eyebrow. "Why don't you check out the rest of the suite? We'll all be living in close quarters for a while."

Jun nodded, then narrowed his eyes at Dietyr. The tone of the bodyguard's commentary didn't have a hint of jealousy or fake cheer. In fact, there was a lilt to Dietyr's last phrase that might have been suggestive. Maybe. Jun didn't know him well enough to be sure. But Dietyr's grin only widened, and any doubts Jun had melted away.

Well, there were some possibilities to consider. Dietyr had the rough-and-rugged kind of handsome going on. Jun wasn't celibate by any means—he just did his best not to indulge in trysts that might impact his career. But he was, for all intents and purposes, on a break from his career. So he smiled back at Dietyr.

Neither of them said anything else for the moment. Jun wandered away to the kitchenette nook. An overhead window in the nook showed a view of the waters above them and the bubble curtains rising toward the surface of the waters within the biosphere. There was also a chilling unit to keep things cold, running potable water, and sleek cabinets to store supplies. No heating unit though.

Nirin had explained that any and all cooking that required heat on Daotiem Station was done at central food-service places like the variety of hawker plazas. Fairly standard for a space station. The largest place to acquire cooked food was in the core promenade.

There were two storage cubes sitting on the counter marked with Nirin's ident code. He was guessing she'd ordered some supplies to get them started but also had plans for hot meals. Surely there was delivery.

All the thought about food was making him hungry, so Jun turned away from the kitchen and headed toward the small hallway that led to the sleeping units.

"What's for midday meal?" Dietyr called from the central living area.

Great minds think alike.

Nirin emerged from one of the sleep areas, and Jun froze, not sure if she was going to stop or go past him to return to the living area. She made eye contact with him and paused, then tapped the entryway to one of the other rooms. "We gave you the largest. Did you want some time to yourself?"

Jun opened his mouth and nothing came out. He honestly didn't know. Frustration boiled up and heat burned his cheeks. The moment drew out, long and awkward.

"Food?" Dietyr's voice called.

Nirin's gaze was warm and steady on Jun. She closed the distance between them a little and spoke in a low voice, so Jun barely caught her words. "No worries. Take everything in at your own pace. I'll be out there if you need anything, okay?"

Jun nodded, feeling like even that motion was jerky and hard to control.

Then she was moving past him and into the main area. Relief washed through him, but he also wanted her to come back. He took a half step after her, then considered another but stopped, hearing Dietyr ask about something to eat again and her dry response. Their banter was comfortable— prickly but full of history and friendship. The back-and-forth between them sparked with chemistry, generating energy, whereas he felt so drained, he'd likely suck up all the energy in the near vicinity in his current state. He didn't want to drag anyone down. So he went into his room.

It was easy to fall into routine. He unpacked his carisak, taking various kits out and placing them in the bathroom, in the closet, on the bedside table. The floor at the foot of the bed was clear of furniture, leaving enough space for him to lie on the floor and do stretches or light exercise if he wanted. And there was a skylight of sorts, under water, which looked cool.

His room as a whole was decorated in simple, clean lines

and ultrafine woven fabrics. The floor was covered in the kind of thick, shaggy carpet a person could imagine sinking into with bare feet. Everything was all cool blues and purples with bright white accents. There were curtains at one end, and when he twitched them open, a small alcove was revealed. It was basically a bubble of clear material with a chair in it, allowing him to sit and still feel completely immersed in the water around him. There was a small end table beside the chair. He could read or relax, meditate even, and just exist in this alcove.

It would be peaceful.

The quiet around him felt heavy. The soundproofing around the room was really good, better than the room at the previous hotel. He couldn't hear Dietyr or Nirin. And in the silence, he started to hear echoes of hundreds of concerts, of shouting fans and rushing stage crew, of urgent questions from press and demanding instructions from coaches. Too many memories, too much pressure.

He strode into the bathroom and splashed his face with water. There was a mirror, and the person he saw in the reflection was tired. So damned tired. He didn't want to follow directions anymore. He was tired of making choices based on what his fans or his coaches or the public would think. He was tired of taking whatever brief breaks the staff could give him—because they did their best, but the itinerary and the daily schedule always came first—and he wanted to do things . . . in his own time.

Her voice had been filled with compassion, even though, he was sure, she had no way to know how he was feeling. He hadn't been able to successfully verbalize it to anyone. That was the problem. He couldn't express any of what he was thinking, feeling, in words or music or dance anymore. He was stuck. Frozen.

And she had simply accepted it. Gave him space. Let him know where to find them when he was ready.

He wanted more of that.

This time, he glanced in the mirror and ran his fingers through his hair until he got the tousled look he liked. Then he left the noisy quiet of his room.

CHAPTER 8

DIETYR GRINNED as he heard Jun's footsteps returning from the room they'd given him. It hadn't taken the guy long to come back seeking Nirin's company.

Not that Dietyr could blame him. Nirin drew people in without exerting any pressure. She had this way of creating a space around herself that others simply wanted to be in. Like him, right now. Sure, he could've gone into his own private room and unpacked his things to make the stay more comfortable. But he figured he would leave that for whenever Nirin withdrew into solitude—and she would eventually, he knew from experience. For now, he wanted to enjoy as much time in her general vicinity as possible, even if she was doing her best to ignore his presence.

It'd been a long time since he'd had a reason to be near her. Not that he'd ever needed a reason. On the rare occasion she did return to Daotiem Space Station, he made it his business to find her. She never hid from him, which he figured was the closest he would get to tacit permission until she finally decided to resolve the thing between them. He was a patient hunter. He could play the long game.

Jun stopped just short of entering the main living space, hesitating as he looked between Dietyr, still by the big window, and Nirin, in the kitchen.

"Just in time for snacks." Dietyr gave Jun a welcoming smile and motioned toward the couch and armchairs.

He hoped the younger man was hungry. Both Dietyr and Nirin burned energy at a faster rate than people of standard human stock, so they required a high calorie intake, and their metabolisms were best maintained with frequent meals. Nirin preferred to keep everyone on a team in top condition, ready to respond to any situation that arose, so Dietyr figured she'd be arranging opportunities for them to eat as often as possible. She didn't know how to leave anyone out either, which meant she had planned for snacks to feed Jun as well as herself and Dietyr.

So Dietyr hoped Jun was the type to eat. He'd liked the young man well enough so far. Jun had a way of listening that made you feel heard and a way of looking at you that made you feel like he was focused on only you. But Dietyr wasn't inclined to forgive anyone who hurt Nirin's feelings, however unintentionally, by insulting or making fun of food she might offer. It would be interesting to find out how Jun reacted.

"Don't be alarmed," Nirin said, with a cautious note to her voice as she carried a tray over from the kitchen. "We eat a lot. You don't have to if you don't want to."

She knelt by the low table in the center of the living area and started transferring small dishes from her tray to the table's surface. There were cubes of chilled savory egg custard in clear broth, topped with thin slices of mushrooms, and a small teakettle filled with steaming-hot water from the potable water dispenser, sending roasted-mushroom-scented steam wafting through the air. Squares of tofu sat in a smoky soy sauce soup base, topped with bright green scallions. Bowls of somen noodles followed, and a bowl full of soft-boiled eggs soaked in soy sauce made its way onto the table.

"Wow." Jun approached and leaned forward, breathing deep. "This smells really good."

Good to be around a human who could use his nose, such as it was. Dietyr chuckled.

Nirin shot Dietyr a sharp glance, then rose smoothly. "Go ahead and get started. Don't let the cold stuff get warm or the hot stuff get cold. I'll be right back."

She returned to the kitchen, and Dietyr reached out, snagging a bowl of somen noodles and placing them in front of Jun before retrieving a bowl for himself.

"Thanks," Jun said quietly. He placed a set of chopsticks next to Dietyr before reaching for his own.

Dietyr smiled. "Right back at you."

Nirin returned with her tray reloaded. This time, she set a large plate piled high with daifuku mochi right in front of Dietyr. There were also plain, unstuffed chewy mochi cakes coated with nutty-flavored kinako and a dish of freshly cut fruit. Nirin placed them on the very corner of the table, then nudged a few of the dishes around to make room for another teapot and a few cups for tea. She also had a cylinder of potable water.

"This should tide us over until we can decide on what we want to get for dinner." She sounded satisfied.

Dietyr didn't thank her, because he knew she'd only scowl at him and tell him it wasn't for him specifically. Instead, he opted to show her his appreciation by digging into the food she'd spread in front of them. He nabbed the daifuku mochi first; they were his favorite and she knew it, and he was reasonably sure she'd acquired them for him. As he bit into one, he groaned, the soft chewy mochi filling his mouth. The subtle sweetness of the interior azuki bean paste followed as he chewed slowly. It was chunky, he noticed. Must have been stuffed with tsubuan. She'd definitely gotten them with him in mind then, because she liked the smooth red bean paste better.

"Thank you for preparing snacks," Jun said quietly.

Nirin only nodded and tapped the tabletop. "Eat whatever is tempting."

Jun froze, and the generous portion of somen noodles he'd been lifting to his mouth all slipped off his chopsticks back into his bowl. Dietyr laughed, not caring about the puff of starch he sent up into the air around them from his daifuku. He had a fairly good idea of what might've crossed Jun's mind as tempting just now.

"Dietyr." Nirin scowled at him. "Eat, then breathe. No sending your food across the room."

"Mm-hmm." Dietyr reached for some of the savory bites, still grinning.

Nirin might or might not have realized what she'd said or how it could've been interpreted. She had a knack for being almost willfully clueless. Since his favorite shade of dusky rose wasn't coloring her cheeks at the moment, he was guessing she hadn't caught on.

There was a lot of potential for fun in the room, even if neither Nirin nor Jun became aware of just how attracted they all were to one another. Dietyr had enough of a sense of humor to enjoy it all and maybe hope for more. He wouldn't attempt to push anyone in that direction. But he sure wouldn't mind if the two of them fell into his bed.

"Since we're all here, let's talk about how we're going to work together." Nirin had settled into an armchair with her legs folded in front of her and was nibbling on and off at the various foods she'd put out.

She had started with the savories, like she always had in the past, but still seemed to like varying each bite for new tastes and flavors as she ate. She could have gotten her sustenance from standard rations or just a whole lot of the same food, but Nirin got as much stimulation out of variety and flavor as she did out of calories. She needed to change things up to keep herself engaged and interested.

Dietyr wondered if she had ever really acknowledged that was why she liked the contract work of being a mercenary.

Jun placed his bowl down and let his hands fall loosely into his lap, his back straight and his hair falling forward over one eye as he gave Nirin his full attention.

Nirin waved a hand back at the food. "It's okay to keep eating if you're still hungry. We're both still eating too."

Dietyr handed the guy a daifuku mochi. Even if Jun wasn't all that hungry anymore, he could nibble on it and Nirin would keep talking. Jun took it without question, which gave Dietyr a warm, expanding feeling in his chest. It was nice for one person in the room to accept a kind gesture without growling about it.

"You've worked with bodyguards in the past." Nirin sipped at her mushroom broth. "It seems like you're fairly used to having us enter rooms, areas, or vehicles first to conduct advance inspection."

Jun nodded, pointedly taking a bite of daifuku and chewing.

Nirin narrowed her eyes at him, then glanced at Dietyr. Dietyr gave her his best wide-eyed boy-next-door look.

She sighed. "I'll do my best to plan ahead. But I'd like to

hear more about the kinds of things you'd enjoy while you're here recovering."

Oh, well, if Jun was anything like Dietyr, all sorts of commentary might be bubbling up in response. Jun had stopped chewing and swallowed hard. Dietyr decided the safest thing to do was fill his own mouth to keep from making a smart-ass remark. He didn't want to miss whatever Jun said.

Jun finally spoke, slowly. "I'm looking for a couple of things. I want to catch up on sleep and rest where I don't have to worry about people stopping by at all hours of the cycle or fans appearing from every direction."

Dietyr looked around their suite. Nirin had chosen a good place for peace and quiet.

"The majority of your fan demographic are terrestrial beings. I asked Addis," Nirin said. "And your staff has never had the idol group stay in water-based accommodations. So it would be less likely for them to look for you in this biosphere, even if they did somehow find out you were on this space station."

"And more difficult for them to actually come looking for you," Dietyr added. "It's expensive to hire one of those submersibles and requires special approval from station operations. I'd hear about it if anyone unusual made a request. So this location is about as secure as things get here on station for you."

"I appreciate that." Jun paused, then continued: "I also want to have fun, let loose, not worry about someone seeing me outside of the idol persona. I want to go out and do things without making sure I fit whatever image I need for the current promotional campaign. I—honestly, I don't think I know how to be me anymore. I've been an idol so long. I've evolved with my career. It's not as simple as just being *me* without being the idol. It's not like these are separate personalities. I just want to find out if I can be spontaneously random. I don't even know if I can surprise myself anymore."

"The station has a fair share of recreational activities to explore," Dietyr said slowly. "I think we can make plans to try out some of them and determine whether they fill the need. I'm passingly familiar with . . . all of them."

He winked. Nirin rolled her eyes. Jun caught the movement and raised his eyebrows in response, but there was a smile playing around the man's lips, and it wasn't shy.

Dietyr would make a list for Nirin. She hadn't been interested in more than one or two things when she'd lived on Daotiem, but if there was fun to be had, well, he had given it a go.

"Okay, okay, Dietyr is the one in the know for all things fun and potentially ill-advised here on Daotiem." Nirin selected a mochi cake coated in kinako. She took a small bite and chewed it slowly as she thought. "Let's talk more about that, but tomorrow, the first thing on our list is to meet with Nyala before she comes looking."

Ah. Yes. Dietyr lost his smile for the first time since the meal had started. He'd have to come clean about that.

"About the dead body," Nirin started to say.

"I knew her."

"I've met her."

"I recognize her."

They all froze and stared at one another.

Nirin let out a curse. "Seriously? All of us?"

CHAPTER 9

NIRIN PAUSED at the entrance to Sunshine Bois, waiting for either Garek or Grigg to deactivate the security barrier and allow entrance. It didn't take long. She heard the distinct sound of Grigg's slide sandals moving across the floor, but then the door to the entryway slid open to reveal Garek standing with a smile so big, his eyes crinkled with laugh lines. Beyond him, Grigg was waving from behind the brightly lit spritzer counter.

"There's my girl!" Garek held his arms open.

"Thanks for opening up early, Uncle Garek." Nirin stepped into his hug, letting him squeeze her tight enough to adjust half her spine and a couple of ribs. Maybe it was the release of pressure in her vertebrae, but a certain tension left her and she relaxed a fraction.

He let her go and stepped back to look her over. "All in one piece, I see."

She nodded. "And still working."

"Of course." He glanced over her shoulder. "Why don't you do your sweep so we can let Dietyr out of hiding with your client?"

She huffed out a laugh. "He's not hiding. That'd be suspicious here, where every resident knows him. He's just being inconspicuous."

"Uh-huh." He didn't look out over her shoulder again, instead stepping aside so she could begin her sweep of the space inside Sunshine Bois. "We've done some renovations since you were last here."

It'd been a while. Longer than she had intended, really.

"Always upgrading with the latest tech," she said, smiling softly. She wandered inside, allowing her hands to hang loose at her sides, but vigilant for anything amiss.

It wasn't that she didn't trust Uncle Garek and Uncle Grigg, it was that they lived there, and no one could avoid a certain amount of complacency when they'd been secure in a single place for any reasonable amount of time. And they'd been there long enough to become a touchstone of the community. Garek understood her need to be thorough. He'd been a merc for the majority of his life before he'd met Uncle Grigg and decided to create a home for the two of them.

"I like the new tables and seating." She also loved the cylindrical columns filled with streaming bubbles that extended from floor to ceiling, scattered throughout the space.

There were slender columns and columns broad enough in diameter for a humanoid to swim through them. The streams could change in color and bubble density to alter the visual atmosphere. Even better, the bubbles blocked any external surveillance sensors from getting a direct line of sight or sound or a heat signature on any seat in the place.

The seats were arranged around small tables or in conversational groupings, designed to accommodate a variety of physical forms. She found the bright energy of the place to be a refreshing change from some of the edgier bars on the other side of the station. Sunshine Bois operated around the clock. During the "day" on station, they served spritzers enhanced with nutrient supplements. Around happy hour and into the night, they changed over to more recreational beverages.

"This area is clear." She'd been quick but thorough.

There were other areas beyond the initial bubble bar she'd have to look at later. Grigg loved reading, and one of his favorite historical-romance settings was Old Earth. Inspired by some of those settings, they designed and redesigned additional rooms, and their regular patrons loved the ever-changing ambience created by the proprietors. Every time Nirin had stopped in, at least one of the rooms had been renovated. General tourists wouldn't know to request access to those areas, so those rooms were open by invitation of someone who lived on station or Garek and Grigg themselves. It allowed for a more stable sense of community, and in many cases, a place for people to relax without worrying about judgment.

"I'm *so excited* to show you the new rooms!" Grigg gave her a bright smile, his blue eyes sparkling with delight.

He was a space-born Terran, with a slighter frame than Garek's planet-born skeletal structure. His hair was so light a blond, his eyebrows were almost lost against his skin. He loved to travel and had been to various planets back when he'd worked in the hospitality business, so he'd developed adorable pigmented spots across his cheeks and down his forearms. When he got excited, his skin flushed and his freckles became more pronounced. Nirin remembered a time when she'd drawn freckles on her face as a young girl because she'd thought Uncle Grigg's were so charming.

"One of the books I read—it's so hot, *whew*—had this *incredibly* fun meet-cute in what they used to call a 'cat café.'" Grigg spread his palms out and fingers wide as he walked with her to one of the bubble columns set into the wall. "It was a place where refreshments were served in one area and people could play with tiny cat companions in another area! I thought it would be perfect for a space station."

Felines did do well in space—better than many other companion animals one might find on Terran-populated planets.

Garek rolled his eyes. "I said we should start with one. One!"

Well, as far as Nirin knew, cats could thrive as solitary companions to a person.

Grigg wrinkled his nose at Garek, then leaned toward Nirin. "Don't even let him try to convince you he was the one with any kind of restraint here."

She couldn't help it—she leaned to one side and rested her head on Grigg's shoulder briefly. She'd been back in their warmth for a few minutes, and already she was eager to hug them both again. Her two uncles, the found family her parents had chosen, had been entrusted with bringing Nirin up when her parents had to go off station. These two men were her godfathers, as far as legal matters were concerned, and she'd been lucky to have them well beyond the time she reached her majority and no longer had need of legal guardians.

Grigg placed his palm on the bubble column. The bubbles inside spun into a vortex, changing color as a scanner confirmed his biometrics, then the bubble column retracted into the floor. They stepped one at a time into the space revealed, and Nirin raised her eyebrows because it was a tight fit. The column slid back into place before another aperture opened ahead of them and let them into a room painted in shades of blues and greens. It was as if someone had splashed the colors haphazardly across the walls and managed to achieve a balanced, pleasing effect.

Those same walls were covered in shallow shelves and clear tubes at various elevations. There were columns with multilevel platforms in every corner. More seating was available in this room, seats set in more small groupings, and there were mats with plenty of pillows tossed across them in the center floor space. All the chairs, stools, cushions, and pillows were a mix of blues and greens with the occasional accent of white or gray.

And everywhere, literally everywhere, there were cats. Small felines. Dark and light, calico and tabby. There had to be two dozen of the tiny carnivores.

Nirin stopped just inside the entryway. The cats froze and stared at her.

She bit her lip. "I might scare them."

"Tsk." Garek patted her shoulder. "Dietyr has been in here plenty. They're used to him."

"Uh-huh. There's a few fundamental differences between me and Dietyr," Nirin pointed out.

"The cats don't care whether a person has a penis or a vagina, both, or neither. They know a good person when they meet one," Garek insisted. He and Grigg wouldn't have it any other way in Sunshine Bois. Their place was where people could simply be. There were very few caveats or limitations, mostly having to do with the general rule of not killing people. And honestly, that'd been more of a guideline, with extenuating circumstances forgiven. "And not a one of these cats was even a little bit concerned about meeting a large predator when it came to Dietyr."

"I believe you," Nirin said. "But Dietyr is a big-cat theri-anthrope. He shifts into a jaguar. That's like a distant cousin. I'm more concerned about how felines will react to a canine."

Her. She was the one with the canine DNA. She was literally a werewolf of Old Terran legends, created by science for the current space age.

None of the cats had moved yet. She was pretty sure none of them had blinked.

"Well, there's always going to be a little tension on the first meeting," Grigg said slowly. "I've never seen them react like this. But at least they don't dislike you. We've definitely experienced what happens when they don't like someone."

"This is different," Garek agreed.

"Great." She decided there wasn't time for this. "I'll come back for a better introduction later. For now, let me clear the room and we'll move on."

She moved slow, giving the cats time to get out of her way as she checked the space for any threats. They mostly stayed where they were or darted away once she came within arm's reach.

By the time she was done, Grigg and Garek each had a cat in their arms and more winding around their ankles. She shook her head slowly, smiling. She bet this room brought a lot of joy to lonely station personnel. "Clear. And this room really is amazing, Uncle Grigg. I hope I can come by and get to know them all better."

"Yay!" Grigg did a little bounce.

The other rooms took a few more minutes, and Nirin made mental notes as to which ones to show Jun into later. Of course, she intended for her client to have the opportunity to explore them all if they interested him, but there were one or two she thought would particularly catch his attention. It would be fun, she thought, to see him light up with pleasure. He had a way of perking up and leaning into something when his curiosity was piqued, his expression . . .

She should stop that train of thought right there and focus on the meeting ahead of her. The front spritzer bar would be sufficient for Jun to meet with Officer Nyala, but afterward, Nirin thought, it would be good to bring Jun into one of the back areas to decompress. He ought to feel secure with herself and Dietyr nearby, and if he didn't, she could always take him back to their hotel suite.

But she was fairly sure he would find a measure of peace in at least one of the areas Sunshine Bois had to offer. Uncle Garek and Uncle Grigg had created more than a home for the two of them here. They'd created a sanctuary for people like her and Dietyr, people who might not have been accepted as they were in any other facet of their lives.

Most people had their own personal spaces in which to withdraw into themselves. Sunshine Bois was where they could come to safely interact with the rest of the universe.

CHAPTER 10

JUN WAS TIRED. Not physically tired, really. He'd had more sleep the previous night than he'd had cumulatively across any three consecutive nights over the course of the last year. But it hadn't been peaceful. Despite the reassurances Nirin and Dietyr had given him, his stomach had twisted with nervous anticipation for this meeting as he prepared to give his bodyguards' recommended answer to at least one question.

It wasn't like he was going to lie. The discussion with Officer Nyala had gone kind of well, so far. The officer seemed affable enough, and he'd answered every question honestly. He just knew law enforcement hated the answer he would give to that inevitable question.

"Well, I think I've got all the information I need from you regarding your whereabouts," Officer Nyala said, tipping her carapace downward so she could study the notes she'd taken on the wafer-thin data tablet she had cradled in one arm. Her tentacles were arranged to support her so she was resting comfortably opposite him at the small table in the corner of the bubble bar. "I do have some additional questions about the victim."

Jun did his best to relax his posture in spite of the tension starting between his shoulder blades and sneaking up his neck. The question was coming.

"Did you know the victim or recognize them from anywhere?"

Jun maintained direct eye contact, keeping his voice calm and steady. "I would rather not say."

Officer Nyala was still for a moment. Then two of her tentacles rose and began spiraling behind her. "Pardon?"

"I would rather not say," Jun repeated as politely as possible.

Officer Nyala reduced her volume to a hissing whisper. "You are exercising your right to remain silent?"

The effect was more unsettling than if she'd escalated to loud and angry. Jun kept his hands flat on the table as Nirin had warned him to do. He didn't make any moves to get up or look toward anyone else in the bubble bar. He did his very best to keep his heart rate calm. "I've contacted my manager, who will bring the appropriate representation to make a statement to the authorities on my behalf. Until then, I would rather not answer any questions like this."

He wasn't exactly remaining silent. He was being cooperative. He was just holding off on when he was going to cooperate.

Officer Nyala rose on her supporting tentacles, her tablet held close to the underside of her carapace in her two arms. "You stay right here. Enjoy your spritzer. I'm going to have a word with your bodyguard."

"Will do, Officer." Jun leaned forward to take a sip from his drink while looking up at her with his best wide-eyed innocent gaze.

He hadn't missed the way Officer Nyala said "body-guard," singular. It seemed Nyala was very focused on Nirin. He didn't blame the officer, personally, because Nirin's presence filled the space, as it had consistently since he'd first encountered her. Jun deliberately looked around the room for Dietyr. It didn't take more than a second to find him, the bodyguard Officer Nyala wasn't engaging in terse conversation. Dietyr was seated against the wall opposite the entrance, far enough away for most people to consider him out of earshot. Jun suspected both Dietyr and Nirin had augmented hearing, though.

For each thing Jun thought Dietyr and Nirin had in common, they had a contrast too. Their presences, for example. Dietyr had a way of disappearing into the background whenever he stopped moving. Jun suspected it was a skill Dietyr had cultivated, because the man was striking, with his wide shoulders and rangy strength. There was nothing soft about Dietyr, nothing polished. He was carved musculature with rough stubble despite just shaving and callouses toughened from plenty of hands-on work.

As they'd walked through the station's core promenade, Dietyr had drawn his share of attention and left a lot of appreciative sighs in his wake. He was popular, well-known on station and definitely admired. For once, Jun had actually disappeared in the shadows of his bodyguards. No one was going to remember who was walking with Dietyr and Nirin on Daotiem Space Station when everyone was too busy taking interest in Nirin being back, on station, and in Dietyr's company.

They had history, obviously. There was speculation about whether they would get back together. He'd heard people openly placing bets as he and Dietyr had waited for Nirin to clear the bubble bar. And that was just the early morning personnel. If the station was like any other relatively small community Jun had encountered, there would be rumors spreading faster than data transfers across the station by lunch. Dietyr and Nirin. Nirin and Dietyr. Jun was doing his best not to imagine the two of them together but was also wishing they'd let him watch. His dreams had already taken him through several scenarios with each of them and with both of them at the same time, so it was too late to avoid fantasizing in those directions. He wasn't a saint. He had no intention of attempting to stop fantasizing either, so long as he kept his thoughts to himself when he was alone, at night, in his own room. The beginnings of a few sensual refrains teased the edges of his mind when he let those fantasies loose, and he wasn't about to give up any chance at song inspiration when he'd been struggling for so long to write.

Dietyr noticed Jun's regard and quirked an eyebrow in query as their eyes met. Jun only shrugged and gave a faint smile. Hopefully, Dietyr would understand that the conversation with Officer Nyala had gone about as well as any of them could have anticipated.

Dietyr smiled briefly and winked.

Jun took another sip of his drink to hide the flush of pleasure blossoming through his chest, the warmth of it spreading up to his face.

Then Jun took a good look at Dietyr's position, the bubble columns between the two of them, and the seat opposite Jun, where Officer Nyala had been. Jun was relatively certain Dietyr couldn't have had a clear view of both Jun and the officer. Maybe Dietyr had chosen to sit where he could keep an eye on Jun. Or maybe Dietyr had positioned himself where Jun could see him if Jun felt the need for reassurance.

The former was more likely. It was practical and made sense for the bodyguard. But Jun felt a little better imagining that Dietyr had done it for Jun's comfort.

"That's enough for now." Nirin's voice floated over his shoulder.

Jun turned in his seat. He hadn't heard Nirin approaching. She was standing within arm's reach, her expression neutral except for a hint of amusement he thought he saw in her eyes. Officer Nyala loomed over her shoulder, but Nirin seemed to be pointedly focusing on Jun.

"I'm going to take you into one of the other rooms while Officer Nyala asks Dietyr a few questions," Nirin continued. Her tone was matter-of-fact.

As if she'd summoned him, Dietyr was suddenly there. Jun hadn't seen Dietyr get up or cross the distance, but he was sliding into the seat opposite Jun, the one previously occupied by Officer Nyala.

Officer Nyala let out her hissing burble. "Nirin has assured me you won't be leaving the space station. She also accepted my offer to provide additional protection anytime the three of you are in public areas. There's no reason the rest of my questions for you can't wait until your manager arrives with your appropriate representation. Just remember, the sooner we can rule you out as a suspect, the better for everyone involved."

Jun kept his eyes wide and his expression as harmless as possible. He wondered if Nirin had told Officer Nyala who he was. Well, he could ask her in a few minutes, when they were alone.

"Only Officer Nyala is aware of the full details of your identity for the purpose of this investigation," Nirin said in a low voice. Jun stared at her and wondered if she could read minds. Her lips pursed for a moment in a ghost of a smile.

"She will be keeping your identity confidential. No one else but her will know, even when her team provides additional support. She and I are in agreement that this investigation doesn't need to be mucked up with too much outside attention."

"I appreciate that." Jun wasn't exactly sure whether he appreciated Officer Nyala's willingness to keep his identity to herself or Nirin and Officer Nyala's accord regarding the investigation, but he figured both were good in the overall scheme of things.

"If you think of anything else that might be of help, please do keep in mind how much consideration you've been extended and reach out to me immediately." Officer Nyala's tone was severe, but her tentacles weren't spiraling around anymore, and she moved to one side.

"I will." Jun rose from his seat and moved in the direction Nirin indicated with an outstretched arm.

Nirin kept herself positioned physically between him and Officer Nyala as he walked past, which meant he didn't have a lot of room between her and the wall. He did his best to get by, but he brushed past her, and static shocks tingled from his shoulder to the rest of his body, making his heart jump just a little. She didn't seem to notice. She stopped him at a column embedded in the wall and asked, "Do you like cats?"

CHAPTER 11

"THAT WAS UNCHARACTERISTICALLY KIND OF you, Nyala," Dietyr murmured as Jun and Nirin disappeared into Garek and Grigg's new cat-café area.

Officer Nyala let out a hissing burble, a sound Dietyr had learned was her version of a sigh. "It's obvious he didn't see or hear or smell anything. Surveillance and heat signature confirms he was in his room before you and Nirin arrived and all three of you remained in the room once you all entered. We have sensor information on all the rooms in that hallway."

Dietyr sat back, keeping his limbs relaxed even while his palm itched for a weapon of some kind. He reminded himself that Officer Nyala was one of the good ones. He and others on station, including Garek and Grigg, wouldn't have tolerated corrupt law enforcement on Daotiem Space Station. It was an unspoken truth about this community, which was founded predominantly by mercenary retirees who had learned to recognize innocent and evil in the broad variety of their forms. When they settled here for retirement, a home with plenty of safe spaces had been priority number one to establish and maintain. That meant ensuring the balance of power never leaned too far in favor of the corrupt. So yeah, Nyala was one of the good ones.

But she was a fellow predator, and it wasn't easy for her and him to be in the same space under the best of circumstances. The current situation was not anywhere near optimal.

It was challenging enough to keep himself in check with Nirin on station and nearby. He was always at the edge of control with her. But with Jun in the mix, the urge to protect was surging through every fiber of Dietyr's being. He didn't want anyone or anything near Nirin or Jun, especially not a being capable of the kind of carnage Officer Nyala was. Her kind had evolved to become apex predators on her planet of origin. And it was not a peaceful planet.

Dietyr spread his hands open over his thighs, palms down. He would remain calm. He would. Definitely. "So you have what you need to eliminate us as suspects. Why continue the questioning?"

Nyala's tentacles started to wave and coil again, a sign of deep thinking. She set her tablet down and tapped it with the tip of one arm. Her arms were shorter than her tentacles and had suckers along their entire thin length, whereas her tentacles were much longer and thicker with suction cups only near the end. "None of you is willing to volunteer full details on your whereabouts and your knowledge of the deceased. I saw your expressions. Professional as you and Nirin are, both of you studied the body. There was recognition there. I tasted the tension in the air from both of you, even your third, your supposed client."

"He is our client." Dietyr kept his tone pleasant even though he hadn't managed to refrain from responding to the bait. He wouldn't have minded if Jun was their third, but for that, Dietyr and Nirin would've actually had to be an item. Not the reality, at least for the time being.

Nyala flicked a tentacle tip. "All three of you had more than shocked interest when you came upon the scene. I want to know what that 'more' is. So how about it, Dietyr? How much of the truth do you plan to share with me?"

Never all. It just wasn't who Dietyr was, on principle. Maybe it was the feline DNA mixed with his human genetic code.

"You don't have sensor data on the lobby." He hadn't missed how specific Nyala had been earlier about what information she and her people did have. "You don't know exactly when the victim entered, if they were alone or with someone, and when the murder happened. All you have is a body and everyone who was staying in that hotel at the time or passing by out in the station corridor. That's a lot of potential suspects."

Nyala dropped her jaw, baring teeth. "Truth, but all truth that belongs to me, cat-shifter. Give me yours."

Dietyr grinned back at her, baring his own fangs. "The way the victim was murdered was not my signature killing style. And from where I stood, the meat smelled bad. Wrong. I've never encountered the scent before, not even when I met the victim at least a standard year ago. The victim was alive when we parted ways back then, in good health and very satisfied, I might add."

He figured Nyala knew. Otherwise, Nyala wouldn't bother to push him. And if she didn't know previously, she would find out. So this was a truth that wasn't worth with-holding. Rather than allowing discovery to cast suspicion on him, he was going to control the way the information came out.

Nyala tapped the tip of her arm against the tablet again

and then lifted it with another arm. She started to take notes. "You admit to having known the victim."

"No crime in that." Dietyr wasn't alarmed, but he watched Nyala carefully, keeping track of all her tentacles.

"Do you remember the exact date you met her?" Nyala asked.

"No, but I could get back to you on that. I don't mark every liaison in my schedule, but I do keep notes of when I interact with anyone from off station. You never know when you're going to need to remember them." This particular situation wasn't one he'd had in mind, but it also wasn't one he hadn't ever thought might occur.

Another hissing burble. "What was the nature of your relationship with the victim?"

"Sex." Dietyr shrugged. "We kept each other company for one complete day, in a hostel. I'll give you the time stamps and the hotel charge on my account after we complete our discussion here and I have a chance to access my digital records. Depending on the hostel data-record policy, they might even have the surveillance-sensor data to corroborate. I'll check for you, if you like."

"That's it?" Nyala asked. The question held no inflection to indicate judgment. The officer was just taking notes.

Dietyr decided to take the question as it came, with no implied criticism. "She was a traveler, passing through. We get those on the daily. It would've struck me as more unusual if Daotiem had been her actual destination port. We met at one of the nightclubs on the outer rings of the space station. The chemistry was good on the dance floor, so we checked into a hostel room together."

Nyala nodded, continuing to take notes. "Did you exchange contact information?"

Dietyr shook his head. "Not my style. It's not wise to try

to stay connected with travelers passing through. It's a big universe and there's plenty of choice out there. Why try to hold on to anyone?"

Okay, that last rhetorical question had held an unnecessary tinge of bitterness. Of course he had learned not to try to hold on to anyone. It would only ever make things worse. Look at him and Nirin.

"So you had no idea this woman would be on station again yesterday. No warning. No invitation for another tryst?" There was some disbelief creeping into Nyala's tone.

Dietyr studied the officer. The tentacles were holding still, uncharacteristically so. It was Nyala's tell. She was poised, fishing, ready to ambush prey tempted into taking the bait. The disbelief was intended to get another rise out of him. He smiled and gave her the truth. "No."

"I need you to give me more information, Dietyr." Nyala's tentacles started to curl inward and roll over one another. "I need more to clear each of you and you know it. I'm going easy on your client, so give me a little extra consideration here."

Officer Nyala didn't think any of them was the murderer, Dietyr decided. She was a good-enough officer to maintain professional objectivity if called for and be merciless, even with close friends, if she had to. She had built her career on several water planets and at least one other space station besides Daotiem. She'd encountered a lot of ways for a being to die. And she was calling this a heinous murder.

She wasn't wrong. Dietyr had simply witnessed, and done, worse.

"She liked to dance." He remembered that much. "She didn't like alcohol or other recreationals. She did hydrate with water. No sign she would have been caught up in that kind of altercation. She told me she was traveling for leisure, headed to some fun event. A holo premiere or concert of some type. I got the impression that she was imagining someone else while she was with me."

It hadn't bothered him, much. After all, it was an extremely temporary connection by mutual agreement. Sure, he liked to be in the present with a partner, or partners, of his choosing, but that didn't mean they couldn't fantasize while they were with him.

"Did she give you a name to call her by?" Nyala asked while taking notes again.

Dietyr grimaced. "Going to have to check my notes. It's been at least a standard year and I have an active social life. Whatever name she gave me wasn't one that stuck with me. I'm better with faces."

Nyala curled one arm into a tight knot, then let it unroll slowly. "Get me the data you're promising as soon as possible. I'm giving all three of you a lot of leeway here."

"Why is that?" Dietyr asked, cocking his head to one side. "I do appreciate it, because we're telling the absolute truth when we say we did not murder this person. But I do wonder why you're being so accommodating."

He didn't like favors. Didn't like special treatment. He and Nirin both would've understood if Nyala had threatened more police involvement. Instead, the officer was coordinating with them. Sure, he and Nirin would've found a way to handle the situation, but this was too easy. He didn't want to find himself owing favors without having explicitly agreed to them.

Nyala studied him, silent for a long moment. "I trust my instincts more than most. Even if any of you confessed to this, I'd be certain none of you did this. I need evidence to rule you out."

"Well then." Dietyr placed his hands on the table and

pushed himself to a standing position. "Let me know if you have any other questions, and I'll get back to my job."

Nyala rose as well, sliding her bulk effortlessly to block his way. "You are related to this incident. One of the three of you is. Of that I am equally as sure. Make sure the three of you cooperate with me and my people as agreed."

Dietyr bared his teeth at the order.

Nyala chuckled. "Please."

A nod was all he gave her before walking away.

CHAPTER 12

NIRIN HAD BEEN a mercenary for years now, with training that had prepared her to survive in a number of hostile environments. She specialized in survival, whether on planet, across a variety of climates and ecosystems, or in space, on ships and space stations of various sizes. She had evaded capture countless times, resisted interrogation and worse more often than she wanted to think about, and escaped every situation so far. In fact, she was particularly good at allowing herself to be captured as a means to infiltrate, then escaping with her mission target in custody.

None of those experiences were helping her in this moment, and she had no idea what to do.

Jun sat in the middle of the room, surrounded by cats. They'd all approached him as soon as he'd entered, and his eyes had lit up with delight. He'd folded neatly into a cross-legged position on the floor, and they'd started climbing right into his lap. Some had rubbed against his sides, his back, any part of him they could touch. One had climbed up to his shoulder. There was a particularly adventurous kitten in the hood of his jacket.

Anytime she moved the slightest bit, even shifted her weight from one foot to the other, every one of those felines froze and turned to stare at her.

Disturbing didn't even begin to describe it.

She was a mercenary. A therianthrope, a shape-shifter. She didn't even need a weapon to erase any one of these fuzzy creatures from existence. But faced with this many of them, she was equally certain she wouldn't come out of a confrontation unscathed. Felines were not to be underestimated, no matter how much smaller they were than her. And there was one big cat in particular who she knew from experience could meet her toe-to-toe in a fight, or in bed.

She was trying not to think about him, at the moment. Even if Dietyr was probably going to join them in the room as soon as he finished up his discussion with Officer Nyala.

She refocused her attention on Jun. Some of the shadows had lightened under his eyes, thankfully. But he'd need more than a couple of days to recover, if her guess was right. From a simple physical perspective, it took more than one night's sleep to make up for the kind of sleep deficit Jun had probably been suffering.

He seemed to genuinely be enjoying the cats, petting and cuddling them.

The cats leaned hard into his hands as he crooked his long fingers to scratch behind their ears. She wondered, for a split second, how good it would feel for him to run his fingers through her hair, his hands over the sensitive zones on the sides of her ribs, just under her breasts. Lucky cats.

Because his hands were beautifully shaped. His bone structure gave him a tall frame, which was reinforced by lean musculature. He had a dancer's grace, and she admired his ability to sink seemingly boneless into his sitting position. It looked effortless. But really, his core strength was probably quite good.

Jun was a gorgeous person.

"You can come join us," Jun said, lifting a cat toward her.

The cat's expression seemed to say, "Please don't."

Nirin tipped her head to one side. "Thank you for the invitation, but I'm guessing your new friends might disagree."

She smiled, though, because she'd admit to herself at least that she wasn't likely to decline him in a different context. Sure, she was his bodyguard, but it was arguably safer for a person to engage in such indulgences with their personal security than for security to have to work around the choice of a random stranger.

Jun was watching her, with enough heat in his gaze that she thought he might be considering other context as well. She met his gaze steadily, curious as to what he'd do next.

"If you don't like cats, we can go someplace else," Jun offered after a moment. He placed the cat carefully on the floor. It immediately turned to him and butted his hands with its head in a demand for more petting.

She shook her head. "It's not that I don't like cats. It's that they don't trust me."

And there was more truth to that than Jun probably needed to know.

Jun only tipped his head to one side, maybe mirroring her earlier movement. "Why is that?"

She lifted a shoulder in a quick shrug. "They recognize a predator when they encounter one. I'm a very large hunter, stepping into their territory. That's never an easy first-time interaction."

"When you say predator, you mean something more than human predator, don't you?" Jun asked quietly.

She hesitated. She didn't make her lycanthropy a secret, per se. But she also didn't like to walk around broadcasting it either. Therianthropes were rare across the galaxies, and of those, lycanthropes—werewolves—were only a subset. An added consideration was the nature of therianthropy, at least her kind: not naturally occurring, the product of science and experimentation.

It was hard to trace the exact origin of the process, but the first official data had come from the observations of Kaitlyn Darah. Kaitlyn—or Kat, as she'd included in her notes—had been a student on Triton Moon Base when a hostile takeover had led to her being taken prisoner. A viral vector was used to introduce melanistic-leopard genetic material into her system and included a catalyst to facilitate its merge with her human DNA. Back then, the survival rate of the experiment had been low, and she'd been the only captive to survive. Her mutation had been the most complete in known space at the time. She'd gone on to conduct studies on herself to provide a baseline of information on the therianthropy virus.

Generations later, other therianthropes of human origin had more stories, different ways they'd come to be exposed to the virus. There were countless variants of feline, canid, and reptilian species. They'd been persecuted for a time, hunted by Terran government to be studied, but Kat Darah had set precedent for therianthropes to be recognized as capable of functioning as members of different types of society.

Being a third-generation lycanthrope had its risks, but so did being a mercenary. Nirin navigated her life in much the way she imagined Kat Darah had: living, assessing the path ahead of her, and making the best choices she could at the time, ready to pivot whenever necessary.

But Jun had asked a question, and while she would've shut down the conversation with almost anyone else, Jun was quickly becoming not just anyone. Besides, he needed to be able to place trust in her as his bodyguard. She understood trust, even if she didn't give it easily.

"A major part of me is canine, what Old Terra referred to as a wolf." She watched him carefully, gauging his reaction. While his eyes widened, his expression was all doe-eyed wonder. His pupils didn't dilate significantly, and there was no scent of fear coming from him. The cats around him and in his arms remained relaxed. She continued, "I have heightened senses at all times, as compared to those who are more the strict definition of human. And I have enough control over my body to shape-shift when necessary."

"How does that work?" Jun asked. His question sounded simply curious, fascinated. Still no fear.

She shrugged. "There's a lot of sensations. But mostly, it's about my intent and what I want to do. My brain responds and my body makes the change. Explaining how is a little like explaining how a person tenses and relaxes their muscles, or breathes. Some of it is conscious and some of it is involuntary."

Jun's mouth had dropped open slightly as he nodded, taking in what she told him. Really, it was unnecessary of him to remind her how perfect his lips were. She waited, imagining too easily all the questions piling up inside his head.

"If you have to shift, will you warn me? Do I need to stay out of your way?" The questions popped out of Jun after a moment's consideration. He hurriedly followed up.

"I've read stories, all fiction, about werewolves and vampires and Old Terra mythology. Nothing real. Nothing set in reality."

She resisted the impulse to scrunch up her face as she let go of the dismay she felt thinking about all the mediocre jokes people had made around her because of that kind of fiction—especially the pickup lines. Truly terrible.

Well, at least his questions were fairly practical. "If there's time, I'll warn you. Don't touch a shape-shifter when they're shifting, if you can help it. Changing form hurts. Some therianthropes become more animalistic, with a different thought process and different prioritization in the moment. It's best to stay away and shelter in a safe space. Don't run unless you have no choice. Running incites the prey drive. I have good control, but it's still wise to be careful around me."

She could say the same about Dietyr, but that was his business. She wasn't about to share anything about Dietyr when Dietyr could do so himself.

Jun disentangled one hand from the cats to comb his hair back with his fingers, then grinned sheepishly. "It's probably very rude to ask you to change just so I can see, but I should confess, I kind of hope a situation arises that will give you the opportunity to use all your abilities."

She narrowed her eyes playfully at him. "You really shouldn't hope for that."

Laughter bubbled up inside her. He had a saucy streak to him, like Dietyr, but with a flavor all his own. He was honest and forthright even while he was self-aware enough to know what he wanted might not necessarily be welcome. People like him were rarer than lycanthropes.

CHAPTER 13

"THIS SPACE STATION really does have a little bit of everything." Jun grinned as the strong bass beat of the music thrummed through the cavern-style club deep enough to resonate in his sternum. "This is perfect."

Nirin and Dietyr had to lean in to hear him too—a bonus he hadn't anticipated but was definitely going to enjoy while they were all here.

Dietyr sounded amused as he shouted, "Even interplanetary cruise ships have a few choices for dance and nightlife. This club is geared toward mainstream music popular across the galaxies right now. There's another one for smoother beats and a more relaxed atmosphere, and there's a third one for harder, edgier music on the other side of this level. Let us know if you prefer one of those."

Maybe later. Right now, Jun wanted to dance. How long had it been since he'd let himself move to music for the fun of it? No performance. No rehearsals. No choreography. Just enjoying someone else's music and letting himself get lost in the sound and lights and a dance floor of moving bodies. After a picnic lunch at the core promenade and an afternoon of relaxing in the ocean biome, this was the change of pace he craved.

He walked around the edge of the main dance floor, which was set in the center and a few steps lower than the outer lounge area. The lounge area had a smattering of standing cocktail tables, a bar manned by a fairly high-tech AI bartender, and private booths along the far wall.

It was a fairly standard setup, really. Regardless of the main theme and decor, all the clubs had key elements to provide guests with what they might be looking for in the nightclub experience. It was just a question of the space and how the elements were arranged within it. He'd had fun noting the design of various clubs back in his early trainee days when there was little to no danger of someone recognizing him and mobbing him. His favorite nightclubs were not only the ones that engaged skilled DJs for good music, but ones that provided the right ambience too, which required smart design.

"This place is very cool." Jun took in the scope of the space, designed to make use of multiple levels while still keeping the central dance area open.

The decor incorporated water columns and a large main oceanic tank; aquatics could dance side by side or among the terrestrial dancers on smaller platforms. It was a clever fusion of water and air, indirect lighting and shadows, punctuated with discrete flashes of strobe lights here and there. It was beautiful and edgy, this nightclub.

Nirin flashed him one of her rare smiles. "It is."

He stared at her. "You like this."

She returned his gaze with a raised eyebrow.

He caught an encouraging grin from Dietyr and pressed on. "I thought you'd be the type to avoid loud places like nightclubs, but you like this place. Don't you?"

Nirin actually looked away. "Maybe."

Dietyr laughed, a deep, rolling laugh that rose from his belly. "If she's on station for longer than a full station cycle, this is where she'll be sooner or later."

It was too tempting. Jun snagged the piece of information and took off with it. "Dance with me."

Nirin opened her mouth to respond, but Dietyr beat her to it. "It'd be safer to join him on the dance floor than let him dive into the middle of that alone. I can stay back to monitor the perimeter. Nyala's people are here at the outer walls too."

Jun hadn't spotted any additional security, but then, it hadn't ever been his job. He'd always concentrated on staying close to his bodyguard, and right now, that was exactly what he was proposing.

He held out his hand and gave Nirin his very best bad-boy-challenge look. He was wearing his mask that covered his nose and lower half of his face, but he could do a lot with his eyes. Nirin held out for one long beat, then huffed once in exasperation and placed her hand in his.

Elated, he didn't waste time, turning and tugging her down the steps and onto the dance floor. They joined the mass together, slipping into a space just big enough for them to both move independently but small enough to brush against each other as the crowd surged.

Nirin was dressed for clubbing, wearing a close-fitting black tank under an oversized cropped sweater of some kind of breathable, spider-silk-light fabric and loose pants that hung low at her waist. The top shimmered and shifted color in response to the lighting around them so that she slipped in and out of light and shadow in an almost-mesmerizing way.

He really did need to find out where she got her clothes. For concert or video-shoot reasons, of course.

Nirin leaned in, lifting her face and angling her head so she could speak into his ear. "Are you dancing or staring?"

He turned his head slightly to her, careful not to give in to the temptation to brush his lips over her ear on the way but enjoying the proximity. It was just as well he was wearing a mask. It'd help him resist impulsive actions. That didn't stop him from teasing her though. "You look nothing like a bodyguard tonight but still completely capable of taking down more than half the club just by breaking hearts. I'm taking a moment of appreciation to give you the respect you're due."

"Ha." She withdrew, giving him epic side-eye as she did. But she didn't go far.

She moved with the music as her gaze swept over the people nearest them, still managing to be more attractive than just about anyone else on the dance floor. He decided to allow the sound and the lights seep into him and let himself go, to savor the freedom of just enjoying dancing again. Being on stage was a rush like no other, but it was one that took everything he had and poured it out into the audience. Here, on a dance floor like this, sound resonated inside him and flowed through him, the rush all his.

Nirin smiled again, suddenly, and the beauty of her, here under the lights, took his breath away.

He leaned in this time, and she placed her palm against his chest, not pushing him away, just making physical contact. The heat of her palm seeped through the thin fabric of his shirt and into his skin. He wanted to ask her a specific question but opted for a different one at the last second. "What's got you smiling?"

He felt her smile against his cheek. "You. You look happy and I'm glad."

Her statement rocked him to his core; he wasn't prepared for it. He dipped his head just a little more and placed his hand on her hip, hoping she'd stay close. He'd let her go if she decided to back away again. But just for a moment, he wanted this.

Lie. He wanted more than a moment. A lot more.

Plenty of fans on countless planets across multiple galaxies derived joy from his music, his images, his presence. He and his bandmates had become icons for the fans who loved them. And plenty might say they were happy to see him smile, to hear him laugh, or to read an interview in which he said he'd had fun. But they'd be equally excited over his sadness, his tears, and his suffering of hardships.

It'd been a long time since someone was near enough to him to care whether he was genuinely enjoying himself and to be happy for him.

She stayed, moving with the music, dancing with him. Her palm remained against his chest, and he kept his hand on her hip, holding her close. She'd adjusted her stance so her right leg was just inside his left leg and he could guide them both with light pressure from the inside of his knee.

Her hair was silken against his cheek, and the scent reminded him of fragrant mochi and roasted rice. Comforting, soothing, with the barest hint of sweetness. She was a good follow too, he thought. He'd noticed she had been completely comfortable dancing on her own but was also moving with him easily, responsive to any gentle pressure he applied to shift them a bit with the ebb and flow of the crowd. While she was dancing with him, he didn't feel the press of other dancers entering his space, trying to catch his attention, fishing for a potential partner.

She was, in a way he hadn't anticipated, acting as a different kind of shield.

He wanted her near him, and she seemed to want to be right there with him too. For now. The question was whether she'd consider being near him . . . more.

CHAPTER 14

DIETYR WAS STANDING UNOBTRUSIVELY IN a nook between two columns on a higher level that overlooked the dance floor, keeping watch over Jun—and Nirin. His own clothing mirrored Jun's, especially the mask covering the lower half of his face. Not that he was suddenly unrecognizable to regulars and station personnel who knew him well, but it served as a signal that he wasn't looking for company at the moment. He didn't want to be approached tonight, not when he was focused on keeping the area in and around the dancers safe.

On the dance floor, Nirin's searching gaze met his, and for several heartbeats, his universe stopped. He forced himself to breathe and gave her the slightest nod.

All clear.

No words spoken. No telepathic connection, the way some people in this universe had. Just the understanding they had from years of knowing each other, first as children, then as young and brash mercenaries, and now as professional adults.

She blinked her eyes in a slow confirmation, then

resumed scanning her immediate vicinity as she continued to dance with Jun. Even splitting her attention as she was, she moved with Jun with an easy grace. And she was enjoying herself—Dietyr had known her a long time, long enough to know that even when she wouldn't admit it to herself.

The two of them made for an extremely alluring pair on the dance floor.

Professional. Ha.

There were jobs, and then there was what Dietyr was facing now. Allowing his protective instincts to snap into place on not only his client but his partner too was risky. Protecting a client was a given. But in his youth, he hadn't known what the dangers of mercenary work could be, especially when it came to managing the urges he had to protect Nirin when he rationally knew she could handle herself. His lack of experience had led to him prioritizing her safety over the coordination of their team as a whole. Badly timed arguments led to some almost-terminal mistakes when he'd been new, inexperienced, with too much temper and not enough wisdom. Worse, he'd blamed her for distracting him.

He'd been the one to start the rift between himself and Nirin all those years ago. Being angry at each other helped him take a step back and leave the mercenary team they had both worked with. Exiting left her free to do her work without the risk of him darting in to intervene. That sort of action could lead to unintended consequences, like injury or even death to one or both people.

Better the emotional distance than making the wrong decision at the worst possible moment—and living in the anguish of a universe without her in it.

The music flowed from one song into another, and the crowd screamed. Dietyr chuckled as Jun—having rotated on the dance floor with Nirin enough to face Dietyr—rolled his eyes. Hard.

Ha. Dietyr figured it hit different when your own song came up in the playlist. Especially when the man was obviously burned out on everything about his life. Jun probably wasn't as excited to hear himself right when he was in the middle of getting away from it all.

Jun placed both hands on Nirin's hips and increased the intensity of their dance together. Dietyr wondered if Jun had to concentrate not to follow the performance choreography for his own songs. There had to be a certain amount of muscle memory involved for pop idols, especially idols who'd reached the level of intergalactic fame. From the quick research Dietyr had done since taking this job, he had learned the vocation was grueling, requiring both talent and immense stamina.

This little incognito hiatus Jun was taking was well-earned. And maybe, Dietyr thought, he could think of other ways to keep that immense stamina up.

Not maybe. Definitely.

Jun likely had ideas along the same lines. Dietyr hadn't missed Jun's responses to both him and Nirin. The man had some potent pheromones, and his arousal, even the faint beginnings of it, was noticeable.

Dietyr wasn't opposed. The same reasoning he'd given for coaxing Nirin to dance with Jun applied to other activities. Like now, Dietyr could keep watch.

He shifted his stance, keeping his weight evenly distributed. It was an automatic adjustment, a habit learned from long nights of guard duty, to ensure he didn't settle too much into a single position. He needed to be ready to move at the barest hint of trouble. Not an attitude he needed much as a station engineer, but his time as a mercenary had been more complementary to his core nature. He was what he was, a predatory shape-shifter.

Better to focus on protecting than hunting.

Watching Nirin had never been a hardship, and Jun wasn't an intergalactic idol for no reason. The younger man was bursting with charisma and energy that transmuted from playful effervescence to sultry heat and back with every change in the music. There were any number of dancers out there casting envious glances toward Nirin and Jun, probably wishing to dance with one or the other of them, or both. Nirin and Jun weren't leaving any kind of opening for someone to join though.

Well, that thought hurt more than he'd like to admit.

Before he could rationalize it away, the two of them stepped off the dance floor. To a casual observer, Jun would seem in the lead, walking a step ahead of Nirin and drawing her forward by the hand. Not so though. Nirin was watching Jun's back. It was possible she was lagging a step behind on purpose.

Jun headed straight for Dietyr with her in tow, and something in Dietyr's chest did a flip-flop. Funny, he'd thought he'd killed that thing called a heart.

Jun's forehead was slightly damp with sweat, and his eyes were bright. Honestly, some people didn't perspire, they glistened. Nirin hadn't broken a sweat at all, but her mouth had slipped out of its usual frown, and there might've actually been a smile tucked up in the corner there.

Jun came in close and lifted his face to Dietyr so he could be heard without shouting. "We got lonely without you."

Dietyr's heart almost stopped. No, it did. He just

refrained from clutching his chest and counted himself lucky the damned thing started again.

He glanced at Nirin. Her gaze was steady, and she didn't deny Jun's words. Maybe she hadn't heard him over the music.

"Want a drink? I reserved us a booth." Dietyr didn't wait for a response, just moved. He needed the task to kick his brain back into gear.

Nirin raised an eyebrow, and he gave her his usual grin. The one he used with everyone. The one that covered what he was actually thinking and feeling. Her eyes narrowed, but she didn't comment.

They headed to the booths, specifically his usual spot. It was off to the side and gave a good view of the entire club. Since he was a regular, leaning into his usual behavior drew less attention. And he generally changed company so often, no one was going to comment on whoever he was with tonight . . . except maybe to note he was with Nirin.

The fact that Nirin had been rebuffing him for years was common knowledge on station. The gossip network had probably been in overdrive since this morning anyway. Somebody had to have noticed Nirin and him leaving Sunshine Bois together. It wasn't likely anyone was going to wonder who he and Nirin were with just yet—not while the curiosity about the two of them was fresh.

As they approached the booth, he let his knuckles graze her spine in a ghost of a touch. Let anyone watching freak out about that. She didn't visibly react, but he scented a sharp spice from her. He'd pricked her temper.

She didn't shoot him a look of death, instead sliding into the booth, next to Jun, and calling up the holo interface so he could choose a beverage.

"You're not ordering anything?" Jun asked, his voice raised to carry over the music to both of them.

Ah, not good to stress the singer's vocal cords. Dietyr slid into the booth on the other side of Jun so he wouldn't have to shout. The booth had been designed with sound dampeners to allow anyone seated to communicate in conversational tones. Dietyr touched a control on the holo, and a one-way visual opacity shield shimmered into being around the booth. It wouldn't stop any physical projectiles, but it did give them privacy.

"Safer not to eat or drink anything we can't watch being prepared," Nirin answered to Jun's question. "Standard operating procedure for us when on protective detail."

Even when they'd watch, something could be slipped through to contaminate food or drink. Dietyr had more than one memory of that. But the risk was a lot lower here on Daotiem Space Station, where he and Nirin knew the vendors well.

A mini–server bot zipped up, having deftly navigated the crowded club floors. It traversed the ramp built into the design of the table and came to a stop with a *beep beep boop*, then slid a liquid-filled sphere onto the table. Jun chuckled and tapped the bot twice in acknowledgement, then registered his payment on the bot's ident reader. It beeped again and zipped away.

"I'll just have this one, then." Jun slid his thumb over the top of the sphere, unsealing it to reveal an opening. He removed his mask and took a sip. "It's no fun to be the only one."

"It's our job," Nirin said, her tone matter-of-fact.

Jun's mouth twisted slightly. Dietyr winced. Nirin, ever the socially clueless heartbreaker.

But Jun didn't leave her unchallenged. "The two of you

make it seem like I'm at least enjoyable company. Even if it's a professional illusion, I prefer to be sociable over ignoring the fact that you can't join me in eating or drinking."

"Ah." Nirin paused, looking honestly awkward. "It's not . . . that. You are good company."

Oh, there was a trap there. Dietyr grinned. He didn't feel like saving her from this one.

Jun dipped his chin, looking at her through a few locks of stylishly tousled hair. "Yeah? Did you like dancing with me?"

"Yes." Nirin drew the affirmative out slowly. She might've realized she was being drawn into something more than a light validation. Belatedly.

Sooner than she would have in years past, though. Dietyr leaned his chin onto the heel of his palm, very much enjoying this exchange.

Jun was amping up the charm. He might not have been aware they could detect it, but his interest was becoming clear in his scent too.

"What's the procedure for the intimate activities of a client?" Jun asked, his voice dropping into a lower register.

Nirin kept her mouth shut and glanced at Dietyr. Dietyr studiously scanned the crowd beyond their visual opacity shield. His responsibility was watching the perimeter.

Besides, this was her choice. He wasn't going to keep her from it, but he also wasn't going to aid and abet in pressuring her.

She straightened in her seat a little, donning her professionalism like armor. "If a client wants to pursue intimate activities, we'd need to conduct a background check and physical search, at minimum. It doesn't take long, but it's better to be thorough."

"And is there precedent for a client interested in intimate activities with one or more of their security team?" Jun wasn't deterred by the change in her attitude, but he did lean back a little into Dietyr to give her personal space. Dietyr held his own position, enjoying the closer proximity.

Nirin hesitated. "Yes."

Not her. She'd never allowed herself to be caught up in that, as far as Dietyr knew. It had always been him when it had happened. Maybe other teammates.

Dietyr decided to let a rumble come through to express his interest as he added to the answer for Jun: "It's simpler. No background check required. Just some considerations to location and an understanding as to who is keeping watch and who is . . . otherwise engaged."

"Neither of you is compelled to engage in intimacy by your contracts, are you? It'd be your choice?" Jun had leaned back farther into Dietyr.

Oh, Dietyr liked this man more and more. "Absolutely."

"And is it possible for both of you to be tempted to . . . engage?" Jun's voice had gone rougher and somehow sounded more vulnerable at the same time.

It took courage to extend an invitation.

Dietyr scanned the crowd once again, then met Nirin's gaze past Jun's head. "Yes. In a secure location. Which is not here. If all parties are interested."

That was as far as he was going to go in supporting Jun's invitation. It had to be Nirin's choice. But gods, he wanted. He wanted this bad.

CHAPTER 15

NIRIN LET OUT HER BREATH, slow and steady.

She squashed a sudden desire to bolt rather than face these two. Dietyr's rough-and-rugged form was framing Jun's sculpted physique. The two of them were distinctively different and deliciously attractive. They were, honestly, the most temptation she'd ever encountered. She might've been able to hold out against each of them individually, but together?

Not a chance.

She almost laughed. She'd been afraid of being with Dietyr again. She had to admit it. Afraid of the intensity between them, of changing the careful balance they'd come to over the years, of spinning out of control with him in ways that could cause either of them to lose the edge that made work as a mercenary survivable.

Enter Jun.

There he was, tucked against Dietyr, the both of them looking at her and waiting. He was the catalyst, the chaos factor, the inexplicable something that made the dynamic between her and Dietyr just flexible enough to give her hope while also amping up the intensity in a way that had her trembling with anticipation.

She hadn't said yes yet.

She wanted to. Wanted this. Wanted them.

She parted her lips, intending to say something. Her brain blanked. Dietyr's gray-green eyes grew stormy as her arousal scented the air. But he didn't move—wouldn't move, she was certain—until she gave a clear answer.

It was Jun who moved. He placed his hand, palm up, on the table between them. After a moment, Dietyr did the same, his bigger hand resting palm side up in Jun's.

Every fiber of her being was taut, ready to sing like strings on a musical instrument at the touch of either of their fingertips. Both their fingertips.

She reached out and placed her hand in theirs.

Dietyr's hand closed gently around hers. Jun lifted both their hands and pressed a kiss against her knuckles, brushing his lips over Dietyr's thumb as he did.

Need splashed through her, both hot and cold, energizing.

Jun shifted his hand, leaving hers in Dietyr's as he slid his own up her forearm and over her elbow in a light caress. He continued up her arm, over her shoulder, and down her back, leaning into her space until his face was a hair's breadth away from hers. Her face heated at his proximity as butterfly wings tickled the inside of her chest. But still she hesitated. They were all too exposed here. This was already too much of a lapse in her vigilance, and Jun's safety came first, before anything else.

Dietyr's thumb ran over her knuckles, reminding her he was still holding her hand. She glanced past Jun to Dietyr, and Dietyr only gave her the barest of nods before his gaze swept away and over their surroundings. He had the watch.

Trust had never been the issue between her and Dietyr. It had been her, not trusting her own control. But she could let Dietyr watch over all of them in this moment.

She closed her eyes then and tipped herself over the edge into Jun's kiss. His lips were soft and teasing, the kiss coaxing until she opened for him. His tongue swept in to taste her then, and she tasted him in turn. He kissed like he danced, firmly leading and responsive to her, his hand on her lower back encouraging her to fit her body against him as their kiss deepened.

Oh, this was good. Very good.

Jun ended their kiss with a groan, then dragged his lips down her throat in a searing-hot trail as she gasped for air. Her hand was still in Dietyr's, even as he kept watch through the privacy shield, the pad of his thumb running over the skin on the back of her hand. This was a first for her, being with one person in front of another. And the rest of the club was out there too. Sure, beyond their privacy shield, but there. She hadn't realized how exciting this could be. This contact, one person nearby, more out there unaware despite being right there, all around them.

Jun leaned back, catching his own breath, though he kept his hold around her waist. He looked around them too, a relaxed smile playing on his lips. Clubgoers continued to dance and party around them, enjoying the beats of the music and the mesmerizing lights.

There was an air of restraint to him, even though she could smell his arousal. The three of them were throwing out enough pheromones to drown out the scent of just about anything else in their near vicinity. That was both a heady experience and also not good.

The privacy shield provided some protection from unwanted eyes and even nearby listeners, if they could hear anything over the music. But it didn't provide any kind of protection from projectiles or other physical attacks. Not that they were expecting that kind of thing, but better to be prepared for the worst. Even with Dietyr on alert, they shouldn't continue in this exposed location.

Besides, she wanted Dietyr to be more a part of it, if this thing between the three of them was happening.

"We should go back to the suite." The words tumbled out of her. She'd intended to sound a lot more steady. Ha. Jun's kisses had completely unhinged her. A flurry of ideas fired off inside her head of what else he—and Dietyr—might manage to do to her given the chance.

The three of them needed a secure location. Stat.

"Okay." Jun leaned in to nuzzle her cheek.

"Remember to put your mask back on." She turned into him and pressed her lips to his jawline.

He smelled so good: notes of bright citrus, tangerine blossoms smoothed out with softer notes of water lily, all anchored by earthy cacao. She breathed deep, then pulled free so she could be more present as Dietyr rose from the booth. Jun followed Dietyr, and she brought up the rear of their little group as they made their way around the tiny tables toward the exit.

The dance floor had become packed, a pulsing throng of bodies, everyone brushing up against everyone else. Some faces were lifted to the lights, and others turned into their partners. A quick glance showed groups of people in twos and threes, some larger packs of fives and sixes, but no truly big parties. Nyala's people were still stationed at intervals along the perimeter and at a couple of vantage points on the upper catwalks. Nirin barely registered them as she kept watch for something out of place—not an easy task in an area filled with constantly changing variables.

Her gaze fell on a lone person standing still, but it seemed clear he was just a young man searching the crowd. He moved after a moment, headed for the bar. He'd never looked their way. Then, when Dietyr and Jun had almost made it to the entrance, Nirin stiffened and reached to touch Jun's back. Dietyr must have caught the same sight, because he stopped abruptly at the same time, shifting his bulk to mostly cut off line of sight on Jun. To one side, a person had stopped in their tracks after exiting one of the other music rooms. The woman stared at Dietyr for a long moment. Her eyes held recognition, and her gaze flicked to Nirin for moment, then back to Dietyr. She backed up a step and then bolted for the exit ahead of them.

Nirin clamped down on the urge to chase the woman. Not easy. Instinct pushed at her, demanding she run down prey. And anything fleeing from her declared itself potential prey.

Instead, she lifted her wrist close to her mouth and tapped a connection.

The answer came a split second later. "Nyala here."

Nirin murmured into the comm quickly, relying on the mic to isolate her voice and dampen the background noise. "You're going to want to check your morgue."

"Why? You can't be escorting your client to public venues if you're going to create a body count, Nirin." Officer Nyala's tone was severe. "You can only take a self-defense claim so far."

"No new bodies." Nirin would have chuckled if she wasn't so disturbed. "You're going to want to check and see if your body from that homicide you're investigating is still there."

"I'm still not understanding what you're saying." Nyala also sounded like she was losing her patience.

"Your dead person. We just saw her." Nirin cut to the point. Probably could have earlier, but she was still processing what she'd seen. She'd question her own conclusion, but Dietyr was on high alert too, a living wall, projecting so much animosity that people were giving their tiny group a wide berth. Jun was almost hidden between the two of them. "Someone who looked just like your dead person was alive and here, recognized Dietyr, and ran out of the club. Check the surveillance systems."

Silence. Nyala was probably accessing the surveillance outside the club. Moments later, there was a curse.

"We're headed back to our safe house." Nirin wasn't going to be pulled into the investigation any further than necessary. "Our priority is getting our client to a secure location."

"I'll keep you updated." Nyala didn't argue, for once.

Nirin let the growl she'd been repressing roll up from her chest. "You do that."

CHAPTER 16

SOMETHING HAD CHANGED in the tension between Nirin and Dietyr, but Jun wasn't clear on what it was. They weren't angry with each other, he thought, but aggression emanated from them both in a way that had expedited their getting back to their marine-habitat hideaway. The route had been circuitous, through little-used corridors and anti-gravity tubes, but in the few areas that were highly popu-lated, station inhabitants had given their trio a wide berth.

He was still incredibly turned on by them, but he couldn't ignore the instinctive caution rising up inside him. He didn't want to come across as having second thoughts or any kind of hesitation. The both of them were maybe too good at reading body language, and he thought they might be prone to making assumptions because of it.

He waited patiently in the entryway with Dietyr as Nirin stalked through the spaces of their shared suite, clearing each room systematically. Dietyr was normally a calm presence, but right now, the big man was practically vibrating with alertness and a potential for movement, and maybe violence.

"Clear." Nirin stalked back toward them, her shoulders relaxing a fraction.

"Security outside is confirmed too," Dietyr said quietly from behind Jun. "Did you want to wait for an update from Nyala?"

Jun half turned so he could look from one to the other of them. "What kind of update?"

He must have missed something. Thinking back, he probably had as they were leaving the club. That was when the energy had changed.

Nirin and Dietyr exchanged glances as Dietyr moved forward, gently nudging Jun farther into the suite. Jun scowled but figured it made no sense to stand around in the entryway, so he headed for the couch and sat where there was space for them on either side of him. He enjoyed them both equally near him.

Nirin joined him first, sitting to face him with her legs curled neatly under her. "Saw a familiar face just as we were leaving the club, and it shouldn't have been there."

"Someone I know?" Jun wondered what the odds were that Nirin might have made enemies in her line of work. Probably high, right?

Dietyr arrived with cups of water for each of them. "Could say that. Our mutual acquaintance, the murder victim, was there and looking very alive. She bolted out of the club when she caught sight of me and Nirin. I don't think she registered that we were with someone."

Murder victim. Bolted. Meaning she was moving. Jun struggled to wrap his head around that.

Nirin shrugged, seemingly having let go of some of her agitation. "We were standing in her line of sight and you weren't dressed to catch attention."

"For once," Jun muttered. It was an odd mix of feelings,

experiencing more anxiety at the thought of a super fan finding him and ending his retreat than being concerned about a dead person running around. "It's been a relief to walk around places and not be the one people immediately recognize."

Nirin's gaze settled on him and steadily bored through to the core of him. "Sounds like there's a 'but' tagged onto the end of that thought."

Jun gave her a rueful smile. "I never would've made it as an idol in the first place if I didn't like being the center of attention. It's a hit to the pride not to be the one in a group that people notice first."

Dietyr chuckled. "You say that. Yet, you're the focus of attention for the two of us, and some people might find that unnerving."

Heat bloomed in Jun's chest and traveled down his abs to his groin. "Unnerving? No. Interesting, definitely."

And here they were, back to his invitation. The one they had accepted. He thought.

He reached for one of the cups of water and drank half of it, then placed it carefully back onto the table. "Is this what you both would consider a secure-enough location for . . . what we discussed earlier?"

"As secure a place as can be found on this space station," Dietyr answered, sounding comfortable and also amused.

Nirin huffed. "Yes, this is secure enough. I'm preoccupied with the mystery of the person we all recognize as a murder victim, who isn't actually dead, but it's not my job to track down that particular mystery."

Jun tipped his head sideways. "And you can let a mystery go, just like that?"

To be honest, he was curious about it too. Very. He was

also incredibly horny, and if he had to choose a priority, he was more interested in pursuing the potential situation at hand than running around the station solving a murder.

"My current mission is my priority." Nirin's gaze was as unwavering as her tone was firm. "I'm responsible for your safety."

He studied her. He'd been learning her over the last couple of days, and there was a set to her mouth, the way she was almost biting her lower lip, that made him think there was more going on inside her head at moments like this. "That's all?"

She narrowed her eyes slightly, but a corner of her mouth twitched into a ghost of a smile. "No."

He waited, raising a single eyebrow the way he'd seen her do to Dietyr.

Her lips curved into a real smile. "Officer Nyala can investigate this particular mystery on her own. I think we have other things to explore closer to hand."

Dietyr leaned in closer to Jun. "Agreed."

The rumbling, deep note in that single word sent shivers through Jun. Damn. That voice.

All three of them were silent for a heartbeat, the tension in the air almost palpable. Jun decided that since he'd been the one to extend the invitation, he was the one setting the pace of forward movement, for the moment. Glancing at the barely restrained intensity in Dietyr's expression, Jun might not be taking the lead for long though. And that was all for the good, as far as Jun was concerned.

"I'm tested for sexually transmitted diseases as part of my overall health checks at the beginning and end of every tour I go on, either with my group or solo. Both my last two health checks came back clean." Jun decided matter-of-fact was the way to go here. "I can send the files to your personal databases if needed. I haven't engaged in intimate physical contact with any being since my last check."

Nirin tapped her wrist comm, then opened her hand, palm up, to display a set of data. "I was screened on my return to the station, right before receiving this mission. Scanned for all viruses and bacterial infections known on each of the planets I'd been to and the standard panel of known vectors, including sexually transmitted diseases. No intimate physical contact since."

Dietyr reached past Jun and opened his palm to display his own holo of data next to Nirin's. "I have a standard health check once a year and get a supplementary STD check monthly. My last set of results are from testing done three days before either of you arrived on station. No intimate physical contact in the meantime."

Jun smiled. No hesitation from any of them, no redirection or even a hint of discomfort. It was a big universe, and from galaxy to galaxy, solar system to solar system, even planet to planet, testing was mostly up to individuals. There were standard sets of tests one could take, but it was a source of confidence that each of them had no problem keeping current knowledge of their individual health statuses. Good. Because a person who didn't want to know if they might have contracted a disease was a fucking turnoff.

"Any requests?" Dietyr asked quietly.

Jun had already made his, but this was the kind of thing it was good to confirm. "I want to be with both of you, if you're both willing."

He knew it might be more complicated. They had a prior working relationship, even friendship, and he didn't know if the rumors about them possibly getting back together again were true. It would be easier to join them if they had been lovers in the past. He could have been a guest star, so to speak. He'd accepted that kind of invitation in the past and had plenty of fun. And he'd been possibly more reassured there wouldn't be lingering expectations after the encounter, because the lovers had each other.

"I think, in this moment, I want to take things in increments." Nirin spoke slowly, looking first to Jun, then to Dietyr. "I want contact with both of you, but penetration specifically, one at a time for now."

Jun nodded in agreement. It was safer, too, for them to have more experience with one another before both of them tried to penetrate her at the same time. But a thought crossed his mind; he did have another request. "Do you feel comfortable with me inside you, while I ask Dietyr to be inside me?"

Dietyr stilled next to him, and it might have been Jun's imagination, but the temperature in the very small remaining space between their two bodies ratcheted up a few degrees. But Dietyr didn't say anything.

Nirin looked at each of them, taking in a breath through her nose and releasing it on a single word that was almost a sigh. "Yes."

"Good," Dietyr said, the word filled with all sorts of promises.

Jun watched in fascination as Nirin's eyes dilated slightly, her lips parted, and the tip of her tongue wet her lower lip. Oh yes, he thought; she liked the idea. He was glad, because Dietyr had agreed to fill him and he was very much looking forward to it.

"We're going to need a bed," Dietyr said.

Jun nodded, not taking his eyes off Nirin. "Let's use my room."

The thought of her, spread across the sheets in the room

he'd been using, under the lights that had been giving him so much peace, was tantalizing. His room was the space he felt most comfortable in, the place that felt enough like his that he could invite them into it.

"Okay," she whispered.

CHAPTER 17

NIRIN STEPPED into Jun's room and came to a stop in the clear area at the foot of the bed. Above was a sort of dome looking up into the waters outside their suite. The bubble curtain rose up all around, rushing toward the small pocket of air at the top of the dome. Security buoys were attached to lines anchored at opposite sides of the biosphere, ensuring their safety in this small area, but she could barely pick them out through the rush of bubbles. Instead, what she saw was water and air and light swimming through dark. If this dome had been directly above the bed, she might never sleep as she stared up into it all.

Jun came to a stop behind her, close enough for her to feel his warmth through her clothes, but he didn't touch her. Not yet.

She wanted him to.

She turned to Jun as Dietyr entered and closed the door behind him. Both of them had matching desire and intensity in their eyes, and her heartbeat quickened. Both; she was going to be with them both in this.

Jun's gaze swept up and down her body before returning to lock with hers. "Can I touch you?"

"Yes." She'd intended for her assent to sound assertive, more confident, but it came out as more of a whisper of anticipation.

Jun slid his hand up the side of her neck, his fingertips lighting up her senses at just the barest of contact. He drew his thumb along her jaw until he could tip her chin up, and she let him, parting her lips in invitation. He covered her mouth with his in the softest kiss, taking his time. His tongue swept in to taste her, and she flicked her own alongside his playfully. He smiled against her, and she liked the feel of his lips curving that way in the middle of their kissing.

Dietyr had come around them to stand behind her, moving on silent cat feet despite his bulky station boots in a way only he could manage. As her kiss with Jun ended, Jun looked up, over her head, and leaned forward with his face upturned—his own invitation.

She only had to tilt her head a little to watch Dietyr take Jun's chin between index and thumb to steady him as the two kissed. Her breath caught in her throat as she watched. She'd known Dietyr had lovers in the past. She'd never watched him with one. She might have withdrawn, lacked the nerve to make herself a part of what was building between them, allowed herself to feel left out. But Jun's hand was still at the side of her face, gently cradling her. And Dietyr's free hand was at her elbow, lightly closing her in a circle the two of them made between them. Even while they were enjoying each other, they hadn't forgotten her.

When their kiss ended, Dietyr turned his gaze to her, his lips wet. "Can I have a kiss?"

She nodded this time, not quite able to get a word past

the tightening in her throat, in her whole body. Dietyr dipped his head down, and she turned her face to him, rising on the balls of her feet to meet him. His kiss seared through her, stealing her breath away. If it weren't for Jun wrapping an arm around her waist, and Dietyr's chest behind her back, she would've lost her balance. This was what she'd been too scared to experience with Dietyr one-on-one. He was overwhelming, and she wouldn't have been able to hold on enough to enjoy it, too swept away in the ferocity of the need between them. But she could now, because Jun's touch was there, anchoring her, helping her revel in the taste of Dietyr as their tongues danced.

Dietyr was still kissing her as Jun's hands started to explore, moving over her shoulders and down her back, gripping her rib cage as his thumbs brushed the undersides of her breasts. A groan escaped her, and Dietyr nipped her bottom lip before sealing his mouth over hers again for a deeper kiss. Jun coasted his hands over her hips, pausing over the curve of her behind to squeeze with a firm grip, then ground his own hips against her. The hard length of his erection pressed against her, and she writhed, leaning back into the hard planes of Dietyr's chest for the leverage she needed to press her hips forward to meet Jun. Dietyr broke their kiss, and she gasped.

"I think you're both overdressed, don't you think?" His voice was gruff, his words pitched for both her and Jun to hear. Then his lips brushed over the shell of her ear. "Will you let us help you with that?"

She nodded, swallowed, then reached for her words. "Yes."

Well, one word would have to be enough.

Dietyr dropped his head into the curve of her neck, kissing her under her ear, on her neck, on her collarbone..

He nuzzled into her as he hooked his thumbs into the waistband of her pants, then started to push her pants down. Jun caught her gaze and held it as he knelt slowly, following her pants with that featherlight touch of his fingers down the backs of her thighs, then over her calves, helping her remove her boots and step out of her pants. They'd left her panties on, and she wasn't sure if she was disappointed or excited to find out what they'd do next.

She didn't have to wait long. Jun stood and pulled his own shirt over his head, grinning. Laughter bubbled up inside her. Cheeky boy was gorgeous and he knew it.

It was her turn to ask. "Can I touch you?"

His bright eyes darkened with lust, and his grin widened. "Absolutely."

She placed her hands at his waist, her touch as light as his had been, and traced down the V at his hips briefly before reversing direction and coasting her palms up and over his deliciously defined abs. His eyes half closed, and he groaned. "Tease."

Dietyr chuckled behind her. "You have no idea."

Jun lifted his chin so he could look at Dietyr over her shoulder, his eyelids still heavy in pleasure. "You too."

Dietyr's answering purr filled the room, and she could feel the rumbling vibration of it where his chest pressed against her back.

She was enjoying this: the three of them. The tension was delicious, free of the wariness she'd been holding tight inside herself for longer than she could remember. This was exploration. Mutual chemistry. A rush washing away all the irritation and fatigue that had built up over the endless cycle of mission after mission. It was already this good, and they all still had their clothes on.

Well, most of their clothes. She didn't particularly like

wearing pants when she didn't have to anyway. Jun definitely didn't ever have to wear a shirt around her again if he didn't want to.

Jun opened his eyes fully and looked into hers for a long moment. Then he leaned forward, capturing her mouth for a long kiss. Dietyr slid his hands between the layers of her clothing at her waist, then pressed his palms flat against her rib cage, his fingers spread so his thumbs brushed the undersides of her breasts in an echo of Jun's earlier touch. Then Dietyr lifted his hands to cup her breasts, the pads of his thumbs brushing over the fabric of her shirt until they found her nipples. She whimpered into Jun's mouth, and Dietyr's hands squeezed her breasts in response.

Then Jun's hand slid down her belly and farther to cup her intimately. She gasped as he stroked her, first through the thin fabric of her panties, then—slipping the fabric aside —through her already-wet folds, until he found and circled her clitoris. She let her head fall back with a gasp as her hips bucked with Jun's touch.

Behind her, Dietyr chuckled, ghosting his lips over the side over her neck. "You smell so good. So needy."

Her temper sparked, and she opened her mouth to fire a retort, but he set his teeth against her skin then and her mind went blank. Damn it. He wasn't wrong.

"Tell us what you want." Jun's voice had dropped to an even lower pitch, more assertive than she'd ever heard him. "Let us take care of you."

Stars help her. She opened her eyes and saw them both looking at her, waiting for her response. It mattered to them, both of them, she realized. They were each focused on her in this moment and ready to give her exactly what she needed, maybe anything she asked for. She had never experienced this—not in work or among friends or with a lover—

where everything was paused for her, everyone waiting on what she needed. Always, always, she'd been the one trying to provide, anticipate, fulfill the needs of her clients, her partners, her colleagues.

"Make me feel good," she whispered, looking from Jun to Dietyr. "Please. Until I can't think anymore. Make me come apart."

Dietyr's smile in response was pure joy, and she wondered if he'd been waiting for a moment like this, but he hesitated, making eye contact with Jun.

Jun was smiling too and gave Dietyr a small nod, circling his fingertip around her clit again as he did, so she couldn't help but twitch her hips. His beautiful lips curved in a wicked smile, and she wondered how any of his fans ever thought he might be innocent.

The rumble started again in Dietyr's chest, and she felt as well as heard it, pressed against her back as he was. One hand settled on her hip; the other coasted over the curve of her ass and cupped her from behind. He used his thumb to pull the fabric of her panties over farther, giving him access. He dipped his own fingertip inside her entrance, and she gasped.

It'd been a while for her, and she was so primed for what they were doing to her, what she very much hoped they would do to her.

Dietyr took his time, slowly and gently teasing her entrance, stretching and spreading her own wetness through her folds.

Jun was tickling her delicate flesh in his own version of gentle torture, stroking his fingertip up her slit, then alternating between pressing her clit in a firm nudge and circling the nerve bundle in teasing touches.

She was losing herself in the two of them. There might

have been a part of her that had a ghost of a chance of keeping her wits about her, but she didn't care to find out.

Dietyr growled, setting his teeth against the spot where her neck and shoulder met again. He pressed his finger deeper inside her, then pumped in and out, and she gasped, her muscles clenching him. Jun responded by rubbing her clit firmly and steadily, giving her more pressure and friction.

She called out again, clutching one hand on Jun's shoulder and the other on Dietyr's hip behind her, riding their hands as they each set their own rhythm, maybe taking their cues from her body's responses. She didn't know. She could barely think.

Jun's free hand shoved her sweater up, the motion yanking the strap of her tank down over her shoulder enough to expose one of her breasts. He paused for a long moment, then his mouth closed over her nipple. The sudden wet heat, the teasing pressure of his tongue circling her nipple the same way his finger circled her clit, short-circuited her brain, and she clutched his head, holding his mouth to her breast.

The pleasure crashed through her, and she called out. Dietyr's mouth closed over hers and swallowed her cries as the waves took her under in the most intense orgasm she'd ever experienced.

CHAPTER 18

DIETYR STROKED Nirin through the aftermath of her orgasm, easing her down as he enjoyed the view of Jun gently sucking her breast. His cock twitched as he thought about Jun's mouth and attentions turned to him as well.

These two were so utterly perfect, he was ruined for life, and he wasn't sorry in the least.

Awareness came back to Nirin's eyes, and the smile she gave him was heart-stopping.

Jun was looking up at him too, a few blond strands falling over the younger man's eyes, and there was a hunger there that was barely sated. "You next. What can we do for you?"

Desire streaked through Dietyr, stealing his breath and sending all his available blood supply straight to his cock. Ha. Dietyr considered Jun. The things Dietyr wanted to do. With Jun, for Jun, to Jun. With Nirin, for Nirin, to Nirin. Being here with the both of them, this could be a long, very fun night.

Dietyr had expected Nirin to be giving. She was an intrinsically generous soul and the nurturing type, despite her outwardly rough edges. Lovers expected Dietyr to be the classic alpha type because of his larger build and—it was no secret—how fiercely protective he could get.

But Jun was encouraging each of them to indulge, to ask for what they each wanted. And Jun had invited them into this in the first place, so Dietyr thought it only fitting Jun lead them through this night.

Rather than answering right away, Dietyr gently withdrew his finger from Nirin, pressing a kiss to her temple as she made a small noise at the loss. He reached around Nirin with the same hand and wrapped his fingers around Jun's wrist, then pulled Jun's hand away from between Nirin's legs as well and lifted it to his mouth. As Nirin and Jun watched, Dietyr took Jun's first and middle fingers into his mouth and sucked them clean slowly, savoring the taste of Nirin's pleasure on Jun's skin.

Jun's lips parted, his pupils blowing out wide. Dietyr grinned, letting Jun's fingers go with an audible pop. "Delicious."

The tip of Jun's tongue darted out and wet his lower lip. Dietyr growled, watching Jun's mouth, considering the implied invitation. What could they do for him, indeed?

"I want you both on top of me," Dietyr informed them.

He looked at Nirin. "I want to look up the full length of your body as I drive you wild with my mouth."

And he met Jun's smoldering gaze with one of his own. "And I want your mouth around my cock."

A slow smile spread over Jun's face, and the man even licked his lips. "I like this idea."

Dietyr's cock jumped in anticipation.

Nirin placed her hands on either side of Jun's face and pulled him into a kiss. Jun wrapped his arms around her, and Dietyr took the moment to step back and divest himself of his own clothing. He stepped to the bed and sat down, enjoying the view as the two of them helped each other remove the rest of their garments. The two of them moved like the dancers they were, this dance infinitely more intimate, and he was exponentially happier watching them because he knew what was in store for all three of them next.

Naked, Nirin turned to him and stepped within arm's reach. A hint of uncertainty flashed across her features, and he almost took it as resistance, but then she said, "I'm not exactly sure how you want me."

He smiled. So it wasn't that she didn't want to, only that she didn't know how to come to him. He pushed back on the bed until he could lie full-length with his head closer to the headboard, then he held out a hand to her. She crawled onto the bed with him, almost stalking him the way a cat would, or a wolf. He urged her close, then coaxed her to straddle his face.

Jun had been at the foot of the bed, waiting and coasting his palm along the inside of Dietyr's leg. Smart. It let Dietyr know exactly where Jun was and teased him as he went. Dietyr breathed a puff of hot air against Nirin's still-wet skin as he waited for Jun to settle into position between his legs. When Jun wrapped one hand around Dietyr's cock, Dietyr took Nirin's behind in his own hands and squeezed.

Jun chuckled and then rubbed his thumb over the head of Dietyr's cock, and Dietyr groaned. Jun knew exactly what he was doing. Fuck.

Dietyr drew his tongue up Nirin's slit in a long lick, enjoying her gasp. She was beautiful on her knees above him. Her belly was tight with anticipation, and her breasts hung heavy with her arousal. The light from the water outside the room played across her skin, and her breath was ragged already. This was going to be fun.

Jun tightened his fist around Dietyr's shaft, and Dietyr groaned, darting his tongue into Nirin's core as deep as he could. Her hips bucked in his hands, and he smiled against her flesh. He nibbled and licked, exploring her folds, taking his time, enjoying the taste of her as she braced herself against the headboard, lost in the pleasure he was giving her. Meanwhile, Jun was laving his tongue up and down Dietyr's length, sucking his tip, and doing an amazing job of pulling Dietyr to the edge.

Jun must have been using Nirin's needy whimpers and gasps as a gauge for when to increase the intensity, because she was panting and clutching the headboard by the time Jun took Dietyr's cock in so deep, the tip bumped the back of Jun's throat.

Dietyr jerked his hips and groaned into Nirin's flesh, grazing her clit with his teeth. It was a race to see who could drive who to orgasm first, and as far as Dietyr was concerned, he had plans for what came next, and who.

He darted his tongue as deep inside Nirin as he could, then gave her a long, slow lick the entire length of her slit. As she started to relax into the sensation with a happy sigh, he closed his mouth over her clit and sucked. The muscles in her behind tightened as she arched her back, pressing her breasts into the headboard, and she flew apart. It was all he could do to keep hold of her bucking hips and lick her through her second orgasm while Jun gave him the best deep throat he'd had in . . . Shit, he couldn't remember better.

Nirin started to collapse, and he eased her onto the bed beside him, sitting up partially to caress the back of Jun's head. Locks of Jun's hair had fallen over his eyes again, and the man hummed as he focused on working his lips around Dietyr's length. Dietyr shivered at the extra sensation. He moved his hand to grip the younger man at the nape of his neck. Jun's eyelids fluttered as he uttered a groan around Dietyr's dick.

"You're so good," Dietyr muttered, pulling Jun up and into a brutal kiss. Their teeth clashed as their tongues tangled. "I think it's time we give you what you need."

Jun stared at him, eyes almost feral. "Yes."

Dietyr reached over to the bedside table, triggering the sensor for a drawer to slide silently open. He pulled out two containers: spray-on condoms and lube. Every hotel and hostel on station provided them, and this particular property had quality product. He applied the spray-on condom to Jun's erection first. The man had a glorious cock, and Dietyr definitely planned to have Jun in his mouth another time.

He turned to Nirin, who'd been catching her breath and watching them both. She was relaxed, with a happy glow about her, and he smirked, knowing he and Jun had done this to her. There was still hunger in her eyes as she looked at them both though. Good.

"Are you ready, love?" He directed the question at her. "Do you want him inside you?"

She bit her lower lip. "Yes."

Jun reached out, taking hold of her behind the knees, and pulled her closer to him in a smooth motion. Dietyr appreciated the play of muscles across Jun's back as he did. The man's lean physique had a supple strength to it, well-defined and utterly lickable.

Dietyr watched, smiling, as Jun steadied himself between her legs, holding his cock in one hand as he dragged his tip up her slit. "You want this?"

Her hands grabbed the comforter on either side of her as her eyes rolled up. She must have been exquisitely sensitive at this point. She gasped, "Yes!"

Jun entered her in a slow, careful slide. Dietyr stroked the outside of Nirin's thigh as Jun settled between her legs. Dietyr appreciated the flex of Jun's ass as the younger man buried himself inside her, balls deep. The both of them were breathing hard. Dietyr leaned forward and pressed a kiss to the base of Jun's spine, then drew his tongue up in a long, hot lick. It was Jun's turn to groan and grind his hips forward into Nirin. She made a muffled sound of pleasure.

These two, they were going to be the death of him. They were so damned perfect.

"Dietyr," Jun called. "You too. I wanted you too."

Dietyr froze, studying him as Jun drew back and slowly plunged into Nirin again. She sighed, drawing her heel up along the back of Jun's leg. "You're sure?"

"Fuck yes." Jun turned to spear Dietyr with that feral look. "I know exactly how big you are. I just had you in my mouth, and now I want you fucking me. Please."

That last word was a plea Dietyr couldn't resist. He palmed Jun's behind, enjoying the way the muscles tightened under his hand. Then he reached for the lube. He coated his fingers, then dipped them down to press against Jun's hole, making sure to generously coat the area as he massaged the tight muscles.

Nirin was watching him over Jun's shoulder, her eyelids at half-mast and her gaze molten. Jun shuddered beneath him, burying his face in Nirin's shoulder as he muttered incoherent encouragements, continuing to move inside Nirin in slow, deep strokes.

Dietyr took his time preparing Jun, pressing his fingers inside him, gently stretching him, making sure there was plenty of lube. He also sprayed a condom over his own length. When Dietyr curled a hand over Jun's hip to steady him and positioned the head of his cock at Jun's entry, both Jun and Nirin froze, holding their breaths.

"Breathe," Dietyr ordered them. "Both of you."

Then he pressed into Jun, carefully. Jun moaned, slowly stretching around Dietyr.

So tight and so damned good.

Dietyr grit his teeth, reaching for control. He made himself grind out his next words. "Move for us, Jun. Take us the way you want us."

Jun pushed back on Dietyr's cock, taking more of Dietyr's length into him, then tilted his hips forward, filling Nirin. She gasped as he did, and Dietyr leaned forward over Jun, pinning Nirin's hand with his free hand. She opened her hand for him, interlocked their fingers, then Jun took them both. Jun reached behind to grab Dietyr's thigh, and the three of them found a rhythm, moving together. Dietyr lost himself in their moans and soft sighs.

Jun was the one to pick up the pace, tightening his grip on Dietyr and plunging faster into Nirin. Her breath caught and her eyes flew open, her head pressing into the pillows as she arched her back. Dietyr cursed, struggling to hang on. He wasn't going to last much longer. Jun was tightening around him with every stroke.

Nirin came apart first, cresting to orgasm with a cry. Jun grunted as she bucked under him, then jerked and came, a moment behind her. He clenched hard around Dietyr at the same time, pulling Dietyr over the edge and drawing a rough shout from Dietyr as he came too.

They held on to one another for a long moment, their hearts racing and breathing ragged. Dietyr braced over Jun, braced over Nirin. Very carefully, Dietyr disentangled himself. After stepping off the bed, he headed for the bathroom. He grabbed a washcloth and quickly cleaned himself, disposed of the condom, then grabbed three more hand towels and dampened them before returning to his lovers.

Jun had tipped to the far side of the bed, on Nirin's right, his arm slung across her waist. Dietyr met Nirin's gaze and leaned in to kiss her, long and lazy, before he handed her a damp hand towel. Jun pushed himself up on one elbow and took the other two. Once they were all cleaned up, Nirin pulled down the covers on the bed and they all tucked between the sheets.

Dietyr rumbled in contentment as he curled around the two of them, curled around each other.

When Nirin's wrist comm chimed an urgent alert, he snarled. Nirin's head popped up, her hair in a tumbled mess all around her face. He was slightly mollified because he could smugly say he and Jun had done that to her.

Then Nirin started to scramble out of bed.

Jun blinked blearily. "What?"

"Nyala wants us to take another look at a body." Nirin just about fell off the side of the bed.

"We already identified the victim." Dietyr's contentment turned to a growl again.

Nirin shook her head. "It's a different body."

"What do we have to do with it then?"

"It's sort of the same victim."

CHAPTER 19

"SHOULD I BE HERE?" Jun asked.

The three of them were standing in the middle of a morgue, which he had to admit was one of the few places he could never have imagined finding himself, alive. Well, there was one he'd been to before, in the music video his group made when they took to more sinister vibes in a comeback a couple of years ago. The narrative video had followed each of the protagonists as they proved they weren't serial killers, and one of them had worked in a funeral home that was a family business. The morgue hadn't looked like this one, though.

There were five tables evenly spaced through the center of the room. The far wall held a honeycomb of compartments, one of which was open, a platform extended to reveal a humanoid body. On the nearest table was another corpse. Jun shivered as he studied the two heads.

Both bodies had the same face, and there was definitely something off about both of them.

"Same height, same weight, same hair and eye color,"

Nyala was saying while perched on several of her tentacles as she held a tablet between two arms.

"Twins?" Dietyr asked.

"Possibly triplets. This looks just like the person we spotted at the club," murmured Nirin. "Uncommon, outside of clone colonies, but not unheard of. But clone colonies aren't a thing anymore. Terrans stopped the practice a long time ago."

Jun looked from one body to the other, his heart beating harder inside his chest. Conceived siblings or clones. Either way, did it matter? Both people had died, and it seemed pretty obvious, even to his unprofessional observations, that both deaths had been untimely.

Jun swallowed and did his best to remember to breathe through his mouth as Nirin had advised. He'd had no idea what a dead body smelled like prior to walking into the morgue, and he didn't want to think about it too hard. He was glad the room's temperature was kept low; it might have smelled worse if the room had been warmer. But there was a musky sort of scent, a combination of sulfur and ammonia. He wasn't sure human variants smelled like that when they died.

"Still trying to track down the person you encountered," said Officer Nyala. "My people were distracted by the discovery of this second body in a corridor close to the club, just before you called in your report."

"You haven't conducted autopsy?" Dietyr leaned forward, sniffing the air over the corpse on the table. His hands were at his sides, and he seemed to take care not to touch the body.

Officer Nyala hissed. "Coroner hadn't had the chance to conduct a full formal examination yet. Both bodies are scheduled for tomorrow. But I wanted to show you some-thing about them before the official autopsy."

Nirin and Dietyr shared a look, then Nirin said quietly, "You're supposed to be leaving Jun out of this. His manager is in transit."

Jun stepped forward, putting himself directly next to Nirin. Dietyr slid back behind Jun. "Is it just me or is some-thing wrong with the bodies?"

Everyone else in the room fell silent. Multiple tentacles were slowly curling and waving behind Officer Nyala's main body. Jun didn't know enough about her physiology to be sure, but he got the impression she was agitated. Very much so.

When no one said anything, he let out a frustrated huff. "Look, we're already here, and I don't have a lot of experi-ence with dead bodies of any origin but that doesn't look right."

The body on the table was the easiest to examine, espe-cially from a small distance away. He had no desire for a closer look. He'd always thought a dead person would look like they were asleep, absent the rise and fall of their chest from not breathing.

This person was sort of flattened, like a deflated balloon of flesh and muscle. It was less noticeable in some places—like the arms and legs, or anywhere it seemed big muscle groups were filling out the body—but the head and chest were collapsed, nothing holding the shape a human would normally have.

A random thought crossed his mind. Maybe the urban legend about seven rodents in a human suit was actually a thing. A tickle hit the back of his throat, and he coughed to resist the urge to give in to actual hysterical laughter.

Officer Nyala sighed. "Initial examination noted that there doesn't seem to be any bones in either body."

"None?" Dietyr growled.

Actually growled. Jun was getting used to that.

"What about internal organs?" Nirin tipped her head to the side, a note of mild curiosity in her voice.

"Not that we could tell." Officer Nyala's tentacles lashed the air behind her. "Both bodies have a wound on the back, from the nape of the neck down to the anal orifice. The killer may have . . . deboned each victim and removed organs that way."

Jun's stomach flopped and twisted. He placed both his hands flat over his belly and thanked his lucky stars he still had insides. He swallowed carefully and looked around for a disposal bin or sink or something. Nausea was rising, and he could taste the burning sour of bile in his throat.

Nirin took hold of his wrist and gave him a gentle tug, turning him to face away from the bodies. Dietyr stood firm where he'd been, so Jun suddenly faced Dietyr's chest.

"Breathe through your mouth," Nirin reminded him, her lips brushing the upper shell of his ear. The very slight contact grounded him somehow.

Dietyr placed his hand on the back of Jun's head; clever fingers found the base of Jun's skull and massaged the tight muscles there. Jun leaned forward until his forehead rested against Dietyr's broad chest. As he breathed, the other man's scent filled his mouth and nostrils, chasing away the chemical smell of the room. The steady beat of Dietyr's heart banished the garbled white noise in Jun's ears, and calm came soon after.

They were both here with him. He was safe. This was something they could handle. They might've seen worse. So this, here, where nothing could harm him, was something he could handle too.

Nirin was talking. "You know none of us had the opportunity to do this. Station surveillance proves we were all together when both deaths occurred. The first murder, we were all in a private hotel room. Fine. You had reason to question us. But this second one? You're saying it happened when station surveillance shows us very publicly at a dance club with your own officers providing backup security. This wasn't any of us. There's no need to subject Jun to this anymore."

Jun straightened, and Dietyr's hand fell away, leaving a cool void. Jun missed Dietyr's touch immediately but forced himself to turn to face Officer Nyala again. He stayed close enough to Dietyr to feel the comforting heat of his lover at his back though. "Is it possible this is happening because I'm here?"

He had come to Daotiem Station because Addis had sent him here. His manager had put him on the first available private transport, and Jun hadn't even asked what his destination was, just ensured it was not where he'd been. It was incredibly unlikely any celebrity would choose this place as a vacation spot.

But a part of the success he and his bandmates shared was the notoriety. They'd lived in the public eye with painfully little privacy. No matter what lengths planets or space installations took to keep the group's hotels or travel plans secret, fans figured out how to find them. It had been too wishful to think he would be free of discovery here, even at the edge of space. Despair welled up inside him and dragged at his shoulders until he felt heavy.

A light touch sent tingles across the back of his hand. He looked down and found Nirin brushing her knuckles over his skin. She was still looking at Officer Nyala, her head held high and her posture straight. But somehow, she was every bit as present and close as Dietyr was.

Officer Nyala made a clicking noise. "We think the sightings in proximity to your location in both instances suggest a link. You might not be responsible, but you could become a target."

"I think we've got the information you wanted us to have," Nirin said quietly. "We're done here."

Dietyr growled. "I'm disappointed in you, Nyala."

"As contracted private security, you have the right to protect and defend your client, Nirin." Officer Nyala didn't sound threatening at all. If anything, she sounded pleased. "My request is that you ensure no innocent bystanders get involved."

"Nyala." Nirin's tone was even softer and had gone cold enough to send shivers down Jun's back. The promise of violence hung in the room between the three of them and Officer Nyala. "You shouldn't have asked Jun here as bait."

CHAPTER 20

NIRIN WAS LIVID. Her temper shot straight to hot anger, then began quickly plummeting into the frigid calm she embraced when she was about to take serious action. The kind that led to terrible things.

Murderer on the loose or not, Nyala had endangered someone Nirin committed to protecting.

Had coaxed Jun out, using his connection to Nirin and Dietyr.

Had deliberately endangered someone Nirin cared about.

And it was a damned shame Officer Nyala probably believed she'd done the right thing, trusted in all her own reasons for doing this. After all, Jun had bodyguards—two very good ones—to protect him. Drawing out the murderer could save the lives of future victims. Nyala had made a potentially difficult choice, based on questionable rationale.

Well, Nirin would make choices as well. Because yes, understanding the perspective of others around her was a part of what made her a decent human being. But not letting them off the hook for their what-the-fuckery was what made Nirin a good mercenary.

Officer Nyala had broken trust, and Nirin had a long memory.

She made eye contact with each of her companions, then started walking out of the room and down the corridor toward the only exit from the police complex. They couldn't go back to their suite, even by a circuitous route. They'd already been flushed out, and the police complex within Daotiem Station was centrally located, positioned to be easy for anyone on station to find if they had a need. If the murderer was actively trying to find Jun, they'd likely spotted the trio on their way to or entering the law enforcement facilities.

"Next steps?" Dietyr murmured, his voice pitched low and almost too soft to hear.

Jun was between them, and it was fine if Jun heard them. But there could be listeners around any curve of the corridor.

"All the bodies were found in very public locations." Nirin didn't want to scare Jun, but it was smart for him to have information. "It's possible this serial killer wants the bodies to be found, wants our attention."

Or the murderer didn't care if the bodies were found, which was not a better scenario from their perspective.

"But so far, this killer has been hunting like a bipedal mammal." After all, a high percentage of the population on station and traveling through tended to be humanoid. "We could show Jun some of the areas of Daotiem that were designed for other denizens of the station."

Dietyr remained silent. If he'd had an argument, he would have voiced it, so his silence was agreement in this case. His countenance was calm, but his musk was strong.

He was grappling with aggression, barely leashing his anger. Where Nirin descended into cold, calculating calm, Dietyr ran hot with his rage. He was angry about Jun being used as bait too.

It would be best if they went to one of the least crowded areas on station as quickly as possible, someplace easily defensible that didn't rob Jun of the chance to continue enjoying his vacation.

"I'm game for a change of environment," Jun said, his tone light. He looked from Nirin to Dietyr and gave them both a small, somewhat-uncertain smile. "I figure there's a plan coming together. There's no place I can think of safer than with the two of you, so I'll do my best to follow your leads."

His shoulders were tense, and he had shoved his hands deep into the front pockets of his pants. There was no scent of fear, yet. She wasn't sure if it was good or bad that he was placing so much trust in them.

She sighed. "This isn't exactly conducive to the rest and recovery you came here for."

"Actually"—Jun tipped his head to the side—"I'm feeling pretty energized."

She stared at him incredulously.

"I think we've established that a certain amount of fun and excitement would be welcome." Dietyr's voice was still rough with his temper, but there was a hint of a smirk in his commentary, and she refused to look up at his expression.

Jun made a noise of agreement low in his throat.

"This part isn't fun," she insisted.

"Isn't it?" There was challenge in Dietyr's tone.

She scowled.

"Darling!" A familiar voice rang out in the open space of the reception area.

Nirin froze. Seriously? Well, she had called for them.

"No." Jun's voice sounded the way she felt, full of disbelief and definitely not in the mood to deal.

A slow chuckle came from Dietyr. "Oh, this just got way more complicated."

Nirin fought the somewhat-hysterical answering laugh trying to bubble its way up from her chest.

Right in the center of the reception area of Daotiem's police complex stood Addis Fionn, resplendent in an ivory bodysuit with embroidered orange-and-yellow swirling patterns that fit like a second skin. Over the suit was a solid-orange jacquard coat, fitted over their shoulders and across their chest, then narrowing slightly to hug their trim waist before flaring to an asymmetrical skirt that hit just above the knees in front and fell to midcalf in the back. Lace frothed at each wrist, edged with sparkling, eye-catching lights. There was no way anyone had failed to notice Addis' arrival.

Scattered around Addis were six casually dressed people, all wearing face masks and a variety of hats. Nirin let her eyelids fall to half-mast as she scanned the room and the people around Addis. Every one of them had good posture. They all stood with relaxed attitudes, but their weight was evenly distributed over their feet—they were in *poses*. Worse, neon synth fibers peeked out from beneath the hats of at least two of them.

There was nothing they could do. Addis had already called out to her. Every person standing in the area, police officer or civilian, was looking at them.

Nirin strode to Addis until she was in whispering range. "What are you doing?"

"You called." Addis lifted their arms in a flourish. "And I came!"

Their smile could have lit the entire room, even if it had been pitch-dark.

They fluttered their feathered eyelashes at Nirin. "You asked me to make travel arrangements with subtlety, make haste, and take the stealthiest route possible. You didn't even know we'd arrived. Success!"

"Appalled" wasn't the word for what Nirin was. She thought she might have been experiencing a cardiac episode. "For the love of . . . Addis. This is not stealthy. This is not subtle. This is not discreet."

Addis laughed. "Darling, you sweet baby. This *is* all of those things for anyone in my line of work. Really, you spend too much time with shady characters."

Nirin glanced back at Dietyr, but he wasn't going to be any kind of help. He had his fist pressed to his lips and was ready to burst out laughing.

Jun, at least, looked dismayed. But when he made eye contact with Nirin, he gave her a rueful half smile. "It's true."

Addis was here, and they'd brought enough complications to increase the difficulty level of her job by a factor of six. She shook her head, thinking hard about next steps. Forget about the serial killer, they were going to get mobbed as soon as the station population figured out who they all were. Thankfully, there were no image recordings allowed within the police complex except the police's own surveillance.

"We need to get out of here." She grabbed Jun's hand and tugged him, hoping the rest of his group would follow.

Addis fell in beside her, and the rest of them actually did slip into a tight formation behind her. Dietyr hung back to cover the rear without a word. Jun slipped his mask back on.

She led them all out of the police complex, crossing the footbridge over the flowing waterway as they passed the entrance. Water-based station personnel used the network of canals in the station to travel beyond the water-specific biodomes. No mass of people greeted them, for which she thanked every star in the galaxy. If she could just get them to Sunshine Bois, they could regroup in one of the private rooms. Garek and Grigg could keep their place secure at least for a short while, until she could figure out next steps with Dietyr and Addis.

"Wait!" a high-pitched voice called out.

All seven of the idols clumped at her back so fast, she almost stumbled. She spared a quick glance over her shoulder to make sure no one had fallen.

"Oh dear." Addis held one perfectly manicured hand over their mouth.

CHAPTER 21

"THINK IT'S OUR KILLER?" Dietyr hadn't ever met an individual threat Nirin couldn't take one-on-one, but he'd follow Nirin's lead here. With Jun and his entire group out in the open, Nirin might not risk a direct confrontation.

"Worse," Jun muttered from behind them. "I think that's a fan."

Nirin remained silent, staring at the figure approaching them at a fast walk. Bipedal, humanoid. Every article of clothing—from their hoodie and face mask to their loose cargo pants, belt, and boots—was branded with Jun's band logo. They were picking up speed, and their eyes widened as they realized Jun and company weren't retreating back into the police station. They lurched into a clumsy run, and the hoodie fell back.

"I'm thinking the two aren't mutually exclusive." Nirin moved sideways with one arm back to herd Jun with her. "Everyone move, go, stay together. Dietyr, take point."

Jun did as instructed, but the rest of his group moved like a pride of cats. They followed Jun, sort of, but spread out as they did. Dietyr cursed and reached out to yank one or two in tighter as he shot to the front of the group.

Addis had their coat skirt gathered up in their hands and was flapping the fabric as if that would drive the idols like ducklings in the right direction. Nirin let loose a low growl, and the last of them took off after Dietyr and Jun. She turned to face their pursuer.

Police boiled out of the station.

Nyala must've had them on high alert with this kind of confrontation in mind. Trap sprung, and Jun was caught in the middle of it.

"Let's go," Dietyr said to Jun and the rest, pitching his voice just loud enough for them all to hear without drawing the attention of every damned being on the promenade. Hopefully. It was late in the night, there were thankfully not many. "Go. Go. Go."

Jun knew the way to Sunshine Bois. He knew it was their fallback location in an emergency. Dietyr wasn't going to broadcast their destination where any strangers could hear and intercept them.

It was almost going smoothly, even if they were probably a ridiculous sight: Dietyr leading a gaggle of tourists, Addis fluttering at the rear, Nirin slowing down the advance of a hysterical superfan, and police descending in a decidedly overpowered wave of force. It'd be worth getting the security video feed before law enforcement locked it down. Just to be able to see it all again and commit it to memory. Dietyr grinned.

Then one idol tripped. Another, who had been looking back over his shoulder at Nirin, fell over the first idol and slammed into a third. The third let out a yelp as they fell over the low railing and into the waterway.

Dietyr and Jun cursed at the same time. Dietyr grabbed hold of Jun's shoulder. "Don't. If you stop, we all do."

"Lose something, cat?" a deep voice called up from the waterway.

A dark shape had risen from the depths—one of the waterworlders. They had the fallen idol secured with a muscular arm around their waist. The waterworlder had twisted their torso to keep the idol's head above water while their powerful tail still swept from side to side, propelling them through the water to keep pace as Dietyr moved his group along.

Then the lockdown protocols shut the exits from the promenade. Dietyr skidded to a stop. He was about to toss out some clever retort, but a strangled wail cut him short.

"No. Not now. No no no," a high-pitched, strained voice practically cried. Their possible killer, definite superfan, was staggering now. Their mask had been discarded at some point, and Dietyr recognized the face—their dead person. People. One of whom he had spent a night with in the past. The young woman was reaching back over her shoulders with both arms, clawing at something. She forced out a final word. *"Please."*

Someone on the promenade screamed.

Clothing and skin split. Something rose out the back of the still-staggering body. The form was insectoid, the exoskeleton so pale, it was translucent and glistening. Dietyr could make out tissue and blood vessels pulsing beneath the surface. Red eyes were fixed on Nirin, and its long, thin, beak-like mouth lifted toward her.

Nirin stopped backing away, done covering Dietyr's retreat with their charges. Instead, she crouched, unzipped her top, and shifted.

Nirin's transformation was smooth, a reconfiguration of bone and muscle that finished in the space of a second. Maybe two. Nirin had spent long years practicing and had gone through a lot of pain to develop the kind of control she needed to shape-shift that fast. Anyone who looked away and looked back would have missed it and found only a werewolf from Old Terran legends standing there, where she'd once been.

Instead of going full wolf, she had stopped her shift partway between human and wolf, remaining bipedal but now covered in a glorious coat of black fur. The fur was thick and long around her head and neck. Her nose and mouth were extended forward in a muzzle. Her ears had moved higher on her skull and changed to the shape characteristic of a wolf: triangular, cupped, and furred. Her shoulders had grown broader, and her chest expanded. Her arms were more muscular, and her fingers ended in claws.

She rose to her feet and charged.

Seven—no, six—idols suddenly glommed to Dietyr's back.

"Oh my! We haven't even eaten dinner and there's already a show!" Addis clung to Dietyr's arm. They should have known better.

Dietyr struggled to push them all off him so he'd be free to act.

Just before Nirin reached the insect in a human suit, she launched into the air. She landed squarely in the path of the oncoming law enforcement squad and snarled a challenge loud enough to be heard across the promenade.

Officer Nyala slid to a halt, arms and tentacles out to hold back her fellows. Several took a knee, weapons out and trained on Nirin, the suspect, or both.

"What are you doing?" Officer Nyala cried out.

Nirin's jaw fell open, displaying her impressive teeth. "She said 'please.'"

Realization swept through Dietyr as he chased down Nirin's logic. If he hadn't ever wanted to admit he loved this woman before, he would now. How could he not? She had so much heart.

"Guilty people plead for forgiveness all the time." Officer Nyala hissed in frustration. "Step aside, Nirin."

"She's not guilty," Nirin snarled. "Think. Those aren't murder victims in your morgue."

"What are you saying?" Officer Nyala's arms waved in agitation. "Terrible things were done to those people."

"No." Nirin jerked her head to indicate over her shoulder where the insect was still freeing itself of skin and clothing. "Those bodies were cast off. They weren't twins or triplets. It was one person and she isn't dead as long as you all don't kill her."

The insect finally pulled free. The body slumped to the floor, looking every bit like the previous murder victims. Only it hadn't been murder. The insect's exoskeleton changed in shape and color and increased in opacity until the same person was standing there naked. She crouched and started pulling the looser articles of clothing off her cast-off corpse—maybe best to keep referring to it as a body —then covered herself quickly.

"There was no murder." Nirin continued to growl, glaring at the officers who still had their weapons pointed at the young woman and her. The young woman remained silent, wisely stepping closer behind Nirin. "You have nothing with which to charge her unless you want to fine her for leaving her castoffs around the station."

"She's stalking your client," Officer Nyala pointed out.

"No"—the young woman piped up from over Nirin's shoulder—"I was . . . I was following her."

Nirin's ears twitched and lay back in surprise. "Me?"

"You're the one who can help me."

Dietyr scanned the area—everyone in the vicinity wore matching expressions of bemused surprise. Well, at least everyone was confused together.

"You're not chasing after us?" one of the idols called out.

Jun reached out and clamped a hand over his bandmate's mouth.

"No. I mean, I am a fan. Jun's my bias, my favorite." She twisted to look at Dietyr. "And I've been here before. Dietyr might remember a night we had."

One or two of the officers rolled their eyes as if to say, "Of course."

"Hey." Dietyr glared at the officers.

"But Nirin was there when it happened," the young woman continued. "Well, not exactly when it happened. But when I realized what it did to me."

"What happened?" asked Jun.

"Did what to you?" Dietyr put the question out there in quick succession. He couldn't help it. He was too curious. Nirin was too busy keeping the police back with intimidation factor alone to turn and glare at him.

"I was on Dysnomia Station looking to get backstage access to one of E-L337's concerts. It's almost impossible to get. But there's an information broker on Dysnomia Station who can get you anything."

That was not a surprise. Dysnomia Station was legendary in the right networks.

The young woman focused on Nirin. "You were there, checking in and picking up some kind of information for a messenger run. He said you could get access even to restricted solar systems. That you were one of the nice people." She stopped herself. "Wait, no . . ."

Nirin had her fangs bared, jaws open to make a retort, but the girl rushed to rephrase her thought. "He said 'nice' was the wrong word. That you weren't nice. But you were one of the good ones. That you did what you agreed to do and you always kept your clients safe."

Nirin snapped her mouth shut. Dietyr chuckled behind his fist. Well, he could guess which information broker would have known Nirin well enough to be right about that.

The young woman took a deep breath and finished in a rush. "I need you to smuggle me home."

CHAPTER 22

"YOU KNOW you just offered a mercenary a smuggling job right in front of law enforcement, right?" Jun asked.

Garek made a choking sound as he placed a fizzing spritzer in front of the Cicadoidean. That's what they'd learned she called herself and her people. She'd kept her appearance as the humanoid they'd all become familiar with over the last couple of days and now sat hunched at a table in Sunshine Bois with Nirin on one side and Dietyr on the other.

Nirin shot a glare at her uncle, and he prudently withdrew, though he tossed a wink in Jun's direction first. Warmth spread through Jun, and he smiled back. Garek and Grigg had a way of making people feel like family.

Neither of them had so much as blinked when Nirin and Dietyr had herded Jun's entire idol group into their establishment. They'd listened to Nirin's terse request for a private, secure room, and directed most of the group to a suite in the back. Garek and Grigg came in occasionally to get refreshments, and every time the door cycled open, the chaotic melodies of karaoke and random splashing escaped.

Apparently, the suite had a moon pool for access by aquatic residents.

Officer Nyala had taken over the same table she'd used when she questioned Jun, Dietyr, and Nirin before. It was all the same scene, only this time, they were plus one Cicadoidean and facing the questions as a group.

Nirin was still growly, even though she had shifted back to her human form. Officer Nyala had settled on the stool nearest Nirin, all her tentacles and arms tucked close under her carapace. Jun had elected to perch on a stool on the other side of Dietyr, the farthest seat from any of the law enforcement in the room, which was probably for the best. Nirin was taking the lead in dealing with them.

Officer Nyala sighed. "We're here. The threat level has been successfully neutralized. It's time for some answers."

Dietyr chuckled. "Might be the first time I've ever witnessed Nirin having to burst into werewolf form to *de-escalate* a situation."

Jun allowed himself to grin behind his face mask. Sure, Nirin and Dietyr would know he was smiling just from his eyes, but he wasn't the one in the hot seat at the moment. He didn't have to be super concerned about what impressions he was giving.

Nirin looked at the Cicadoidean. "It'd be good to tell us what happened and why. Quickly. Then we can talk about what help you need."

The Cicadoidean nodded, short hair swishing around her jaw as she did. "My name is Maggie. Cicadoideans like me do our traveling in our nymph stage. We're supposed to have plenty of time to wander the galaxies. Decades of active time outside of suspended animation, at least."

Officer Nyala was taking notes again on her data tablet. Jun wondered how much information there was on species like Cicadoideans. It was a big universe, and if Maggie was talking about galaxies, there was no telling how long it had taken her to get to this one.

Maggie took a sip of a spritzer and continued. "I wanted to follow E-L337 on their annual tour, every concert across the different galaxies. It was a once-in-a-lifetime way to explore and enjoy my favorite music group. I was able to get tour passes, but not backstage access."

"Thus the stop at Dysnomia Station," prompted Dietyr.

Maggie nodded. "I figured I could try in between concerts, but then there was an accident at one of the event locations. The venue released pheromones even though those aren't supposed to be a part of the show. The pheromones forced me out of my nymph stage prematurely."

Guilt stabbed at Jun, and he leaned forward. "That was a big issue. After that, our agency wrote into contracts that venues weren't allowed to do that for their concerts anymore, even if it was a common entertainment practice for that culture. Too many tourists arrive from out of system for every show."

"I don't blame E-L337." Maggie gave him a sad smile. "It didn't happen at any of the other concerts, so it was pretty obvious to me it was that venue. But that's why I keep shedding skins. I went back to Dysnomia Station to try to find a way to halt my progression or an early passage home, since my scheduled transport back home isn't for another standard decade at least."

Jun didn't even want to try the math on how many bodies that would be.

"I can choose to stay in nymph stage, which is how I can keep choosing this appearance, but it's not sustainable for much longer." Maggie bit her lip. It was a very human expression for someone who had a long, thin, beak-like mouth in their natural form. "It's taking way too much food to maintain this form with my metabolism, and my molting frequency has gotten worse and worse. I had to reallocate some of my souvenir budget to food purchases."

Jun wondered just how much Maggie had planned to acquire in souvenirs and how much that translated to in food purchases so far. Maybe he could do something to compensate her. He'd have to talk to Addis.

Officer Nyala wrapped an arm over the top of her carapace and emitted a gurgling sound. "You mean you've been leaving bodies across the galaxy while you chased Nirin?"

Maggie lifted her shoulders and managed a sheepish expression. She really had studied human body language well.

"You think I can get you home." Nirin was staring at Maggie.

"The information broker said you reminded him of an old friend and that because you're a lot like her, even if you do shape-change into a wolf and not a panther, you could find a way." Maggie was all earnest faith. "I need to get home. I need my atmosphere, my sun and moons, and my soil for it to be safe to molt and emerge into my adult form."

Exhaustion pulled at Jun as conversation continued about exactly where Maggie's home system was located. He'd gone through a whole lot of emotions in one night and his thoughts were swirling around in a mix with more messy feelings. He knew Nirin was a mercenary and good at what she did, but he actually had no idea what sort of means she had at her disposal. She wasn't the captain of a ship as far as he knew. Neither was Dietyr.

Actually, beyond what they had agreed to in Jun's current contract, he had no idea what they planned to do next. Nor did he know what the relationship between the three of them would be like when he did return to his life as an intergalactic idol.

A cold shiver ran down his back, and his lungs seized up. It was the first time he'd thought about returning. He didn't know how he could and still be with them too. And he wanted to. Wanted to continue to be with them.

Nirin hadn't answered Maggie yet.

Tears were welling up in Maggie's eyes. "Please, please help me get home."

"It's not as if I don't leave this system regularly," Nirin said slowly.

Dietyr growled from his seat next to Jun. Jun thought he might be feeling a similar sentiment. He didn't want Nirin to disappear into the stars. Weren't they still figuring out how far Maggie's home system actually was? There was no telling how long Nirin would be gone or whether their lives would still be in sync by the time she found her way back.

"You've never taken a job that required cold sleep." Dietyr dropped the statement into the middle of the conversation, his tone quiet and devoid of the wry humor Jun had come to enjoy.

Jun froze. They must have pulled the data while he'd been lost in thought. Nausea took over him, roiling his stomach.

It was a serious consideration. Space travel had advanced over the centuries after humankind had stretched beyond the limits of the Terran solar system, but it was a big universe. Some galaxies required cold sleep to get there if there wasn't a wormhole or stargate close enough. That kind of travel had the potential to cut a person off from others of their time. It wasn't recommended for anyone with close family or personal connections.

If Nirin went on a journey that required cold sleep, Dietyr might follow her, and the both of them would wake years or decades later. Their personal chronological age would have been held in stasis. And Jun would have returned to his group, continued singing, and aged. Their lives would be out of sync, not just because of distance.

He sucked his lower lip between his teeth to keep himself from blurting out something stupid, like "no." After all, it wasn't his or anyone else's place to tell Nirin not to help someone or take a contract.

There was something he could do for the immediate situation though. "You said it takes a lot to sustain you while you're . . . shedding like this. I'll cover the cost of your lodging and meals while you're here on station, if you'll allow me."

Maggie's human-shaped hands flew to cover the lower half of her face as her eyes went wide.

"Oh! You don't have to trouble yourself, Jun. Really! This wasn't E-L337." The words came out muffled, and her eyes started glistening as tears welled up. Her whole brand-new human body started to tremble. "You're so nice!"

"It might not have been us who did this to you, but it's the least we can do for a dedicated fan. We'll help you lodge a complaint and a demand for compensation with the venue in the meantime," Jun said with more confidence. He could afford lodging and food for such an extenuating circumstance, and he knew his agency could follow through with the rest. "It'll help as a supplement to the documentation Officer Nyala might have to compile too."

Officer Nyala sighed, waving a tentacle weakly. "Sure. Have your people connect with me. I'll be buried under reports for the foreseeable future anyway."

He suppressed a smirk. He hadn't appreciated being set

up as bait just a couple of hours ago. He'd been more imme-diately focused on Nirin and Dietyr in the moment, but now that the perceived danger had passed, his anger had been slowly simmering.

Officer Nyala would have a special kind of fun answering to his agency for her decision to use an innocent intergalactic super idol for bait in a petty local space station investigation. He'd just put in a word with Addis to ensure the people of Daotiem Space Station didn't suffer for her questionable decisions.

"I don't have any more questions." Officer Nyala stowed her tablet, sounding tired. "No murder. As long as you figure out a way to avoid creating a panic with your . . . molting detritus, we can avoid undue alarm on station."

Nyala rose from the table, balanced on her tentacles, and headed for the exit. In the doorway, she paused and turned back. "My officers will provide support to secure the area for our current guests, Nirin, on your lead."

Nirin stared at Nyala for a long moment, then nodded.

Dietyr sat back, rubbing his chin. "I can work on securing a route back to their transport ship through the engineering tunnels to avoid any further public exposure."

"Sure." Nirin had withdrawn into herself, her face a neutral mask. She was thinking.

Jun felt cut off from her, and that realization was almost physically painful. He must've given some sign in his posture, or made some kind of noise, because her gaze lifted and locked on him.

"It's okay," she whispered softly, and the warmth of her words was a caress. "I'm here. We're all here."

But for how much longer?

CHAPTER 23

NIRIN SIGHED and pressed a fingertip to the space between her brows, then pushed up to relieve the tension gathering at the front of her skull. Dietyr and Jun had gone to join the karaoke pool party in progress in one of the private rooms of Sunshine Bois, but she wasn't ready for that many people yet. Not even to make Jun and Dietyr happy.

"All of that was very exciting!" said Grigg, coming around the counter. He placed a glass in front of her that looked like effervescent sunshine. "One part passion fruit–orange–guava juice cut with three parts sparkling water, just the way you like it."

"Thank you, Uncle Grigg." Honestly, the drink took her back to her tween days when she'd come to Sunshine Bois and had to climb up onto one of their barstools to hang out with her favorite godfathers.

"Definitely exciting." Garek joined them, placing a plate of sliced green mangoes in front of her. It was accompanied by a dip that was spicy, sweet, and savory, made of shallots, hot chili peppers, tiny dried krill, sugar, and fish sauce cooked together just until the flavors melted together —another childhood favorite of hers. "I can count the number of times you've shifted to werewolf form right out in the open on one hand. Even as fast as you are, shape-shifting in public leaves you vulnerable long enough for a sharpshooter to take you out. What made you take the risk, love?"

Nirin picked up a slice and used it to scoop some of the thick dip, then took a big bite and let the sour of the mango dance across her palate with the spicy-sweet umami of the dip. The mango was almost firm enough to crunch as she chewed—perfect—and the flavors lingered, bursting across her tongue and even making the back of her jaw tingle. More tension slid away, and she rolled her shoulders to help her muscles loosen further.

"All of law enforcement was charging us out in the open, thanks to Nyala's planned ambush. The main prome-nade doesn't have any reasonable vantage points for a sniper to aim at the police station." She reached for another slice of mango. "I had a few seconds to stall their charge and couldn't think of something else effective enough to shock them in the moment."

"Fair. You still gave this old man a scare." Garek tipped his head down until his chin was almost touching his chest and glared up at her through eyelashes so fair, they were almost translucent.

The expression had been more severe coming from her father. Maybe it was because her father had sometimes favored antique reading glasses. The glaring over the rims of those was impactful.

"Well"—Grigg placed his hand flat over his chest—"I just about lost a solar decade from my life. It's one thing to know you're going out there and doing serious work. It's a whole different experience watching you in action right out on the main promenade."

They'd never admit it, but Garek and Grigg had to have access to some of the secure live feeds used by station law enforcement to communicate during planned ops. Nirin knew better than to ask about the logistics. Having good information was a part of surviving as a merc and the Sunshine Bois had roots throughout the station community.

Nirin swallowed hard. "I'm sorry."

"Oh, don't be." Garek slapped a hand on the counter-top. "I've never been so proud as when it came out that you saved that poor young person. Who knows what harm could have come with everyone all amped up and thinking she was a serial killer? The situation needed to be de-escalated."

"We're both proud," Grigg confirmed. Then he giggled. "You shifted and growled at the entire law enforcement contingent of Daotiem Station. Intimidated them to a stand-still. They'll say it was a professional courtesy, but we saw it. They thought twice about trying to take you on."

"Dietyr had my back and they knew it," Nirin insisted. Her cheeks were hot with embarrassment, but she was pleased too. She wasn't immune to praise, especially when it came from her two godfathers.

Garek had been a mercenary, like her parents. He'd been to as many places, done as many jobs, survived as many dangerous situations, and more. After all, he was still here, and her parents were not. But that was emotional baggage to unpack some other time. Maybe never. Nirin didn't feel compelled to do so anytime soon.

"Maybe." Grigg gave her a bit of side-eye. "Most people on station forget Dietyr is a shape-shifter too. He's stealthier about it."

"He's a cat," Nirin pointed out. "It's in his nature to be sneaky."

"So what's next?" Garek asked.

Oh, Uncle Garek. He would know she was lingering for another reason besides her own aversion to being around people.

She liked to be independent, self-sufficient. It was *her* contract that led to all this and *her* actions that placed her in this position. It was because she'd been competent, had the skill sets and the strength to bring herself this far. But sometimes it required even more strength to do what she did next. "Can you help me? I was hoping you had some suggestions."

Garek gave her the gentlest smile she could find in all the galaxies she'd been to and back. "Of course, love."

Grigg put an arm around her shoulders and gave her a firm squeeze. "Always."

"Do you want to contract for a job that takes you into cold sleep?" Garek asked.

Nirin shook her head. "No. If I did, I'd have taken one before."

"Mm-hmm." Grigg gave her a knowing grin. "As much as we know you love us, methinks there might have been at least one other reason you wanted to be able to come home once in a while."

Nirin opened her mouth to shoot back a pithy response, then stopped. She tried not to lie to them, ever, even about something she was realizing she'd been lying to herself about for a good long time. Or maybe not lying, per se. Just denying. "Every time I came back, it wasn't the right time for us. Neither of us was in the right place."

Grigg nodded. "I think we all know why now."

It was Garek's turn to grin. "That pop idol is hot. Seriously. You and Dietyr are beautiful people and I love you, but that young man's backside is an intergalactic phenomenon."

She was not going to tell either of her godfathers just how incredible the rest of Jun's physique was. They didn't need to know. But now she was thinking about Jun, and Dietyr, and just how much more intimately familiar she was with the both of them.

Her entire face was flushed. She could feel it.

"People came in gossiping about the three of you together," Grigg leaned in to whisper. As if it wouldn't have been too late already if either Jun or Dietyr had come back out to the juice-spritzer-shop area to find her and heard what her uncles had already said. "You all are a wow kind of combination."

She cleared her throat. "Therefore, no jobs that take me away from the interstellar or intergalactic routes I can reach via wormhole or jumpgate."

"Well, thank stars for that," Garek said. "But you don't have any immediate connections who can take the job, do you?"

She shook her head. Obviously, she'd have reached out to one of them by now if she had. "Of the contacts I have that could and would make the trip, I wouldn't trust any with Maggie."

Garek sighed. "It's always harder when you know their name."

Nirin nodded, though she was softer than she would've ever wanted to admit. She'd promised herself she would help Maggie as soon as Maggie had screamed "please."

Maggie's voice had held the kind of despair that Nirin's shouts inside her own mind had when her parents died. There hadn't been anyone to help her parents then. But

Nirin had the means and the ability to help Maggie now. Maybe it was a tenuous connection, but it was real as far as Nirin was concerned.

Garek tapped his wrist unit, and a holographic display popped up. "Let's start with contacts in the neighboring star systems. There's still a good number of active mercs who owe me favors."

"Thank you," Nirin said quietly.

This was the strength Uncles Garek and Grigg had taught her. She couldn't remember them having ever sat her down and said it in words. But she'd witnessed it day to day, perched on a stool in Sunshine Bois, drinking liquid sunlight. People, connected by ties of comradeship and friendship. Some ties were stronger and deeper than others, sure. But everyone recognized one another's skills and abilities, acknowledged specializations and capacities. Here—where mercenaries came to rest and chat, trade ideas, and sometimes combine thoughts until a better solution presented itself among them—is where she learned that the individual didn't have to be the answer. That sometimes tasks were better shared or delegated to those who were a better fit.

She could make the choice to solve this without being the solution.

Because for once, there was something tugging at her, keeping her. For once, she felt the pull of home, and it was a call for more than just checking in at Daotiem Station. Home was in the embrace of two men who were just a room away. Wherever they went, that's where home would be.

What she couldn't solve for was what she would do if one left and one stayed.

CHAPTER 24

DIETYR HAD KEPT his peace all the way to Sunshine Bois. Kept his commentary to a minimum while they sorted out the mess with Nyala and Maggie. Watched over his lover as he'd reunited with his bandmates. He'd even kept his calm as they escorted the whole sparkling, bubbly mess of them back to the band's transport ship in their secure docking slip. And took the time to toss Maggie on board while they figured out the rest of their plan for her.

Now he had Jun and Nirin back in their hideaway, their space secured inside and out, and he was done with keeping his thoughts and emotions to himself.

"We need to talk."

Nirin paused pulling together snacks in the kitchenette. Jun sat down on the couch and looked at Dietyr, giving Dietyr his full attention.

"There's probably a lot of questions floating right now, and I figure we should ask them all out loud and then answer as many as we can." He wasn't suggesting each person ask a question and get an individual answer; Dietyr wasn't sure that would work in this scenario. They were all too used to burying their wants in favor of what they felt needed to be done in their respective careers.

He dragged a hand through his hair. "I'll start. I like what we've started and I'm done being solo here on station. Do you two want to continue this thing between us all? If you don't that's okay. I'll figure out what I want to do next. But if you do, what are possible next steps for us?"

There. Those were his major questions. He sat down on the couch near Jun but not close enough to imply any kind of pressure.

Jun cleared his throat. "I have the same questions. I have commitments to E-L337 though, and I can't break those. It wouldn't be fair to my bandmates. Is there a path for the three of us that works with my being a part of E-L337? We're on tour almost all the time, and working on albums in between tours. Relationships with idols like me aren't unheard of, but they're hard. Even harder if the partner or partners are long-distance."

They both looked at Nirin. She carried a tray from the kitchen and placed it on the low table in front of the couch. It was a charcuterie board with an array of cured and smoked meats arranged alongside tiny dishes of condiments like stone-ground mustard and bacon jam. She left and returned with a cheese tray and a bowl of a smoked-fish spread. One more trip brought a basket with small loaves of bread and a pot of fragrant tea.

She straightened from depositing all the food on the table and dropped her arms to her sides. Finally, she said, "I'm not going to take Maggie home."

Dietyr's heart jumped into his throat, and he had to swallow hard to speak. Even so, his voice came out a little hoarse. "That . . . wasn't a question."

"But it leads to a question. What do I do now?" Nirin

asked quietly. "I worked with Uncle Garek and Uncle Grigg to find a solution for Maggie. She'll have people I trust to take her back home. I don't have another contract lined up after this one. You both asked questions that I had. So I want to know. What are my options? What do I do now?"

Dietyr leaned forward to rest his elbows on his knees, stippling his fingers together as his hands covered his mouth. He blew out a breath of relief. They all wanted to know if they were staying together.

It was Jun who put it out there in words. "So is it safe to say one answer is that we all want to continue together? Like a relationship?"

"Yes."

Both Nirin and Dietyr had breathed the answer out in unison. All three of them smiled.

Nirin looked at Dietyr. "Jun's got commitments to E-L337. You're a station engineer here. I can find work with either of you, but the long-distance situation is still going to happen."

Dietyr shook his head and made eye contact with Nirin. "I didn't take temporary leave to accept this contract. I'm not a permanent station engineer for Daotiem anymore. I put in my notice and collected severance right after I took this job with you."

Her eyes widened, and her lips parted in surprise.

He grinned, laughter bubbling up from his belly. "I was going to prove to you we could work together. If you didn't accept me, I was going to pick up freelance merc work to try to move on."

Anything would have been better than remaining here on station where so many memories of her were in every nook and cranny of the place.

"So the two of you," Jun said hesitantly. "The two of you can travel."

They both turned to look at him and nodded.

Nirin chuckled. "Addis will probably jump at the chance to add us to the group's permanent security. We'll need to negotiate a fair salary for each of us. They're going to try to get us as a package deal with you as incentive."

Jun grinned. "Maybe. You can make Addis sweat a little bit. I promise not to take their side in negotiations."

Feeling more relaxed, Dietyr leaned back and stretched his arms across the back of the couch. Jun angled himself to face Dietyr, resting his own arm on the back of the couch so their hands touched. Then Jun looked at Nirin and patted the cushion between the two of them.

She regarded them with an enigmatic expression. "Questions answered. We're doing this, together. Next steps, identified."

Jun's brows drew together. "Yeah."

Dietyr cleared his throat, then offered, "And if things change and our relationship or individual needs evolve, we can work on that together too. We should let ourselves evolve with each other. We're giving this a try."

He didn't want her to feel trapped. Presented with a trap, she tended to bolt rather than be caught.

She nodded in acknowledgement, then bent over, unfastened her boots, and stepped out of them.

Okay, she wasn't going to bolt.

He watched, mesmerized, as she unbuttoned and unbuckled various articles of clothing until she had slowly divested herself of every stitch and thread she'd been wearing. Jun had shifted his hand to clutch Dietyr's wrist as Jun watched her too.

"No one said we had to execute next steps right away." Nirin's voice was low and husky, an invitation.

"I'd really like to get back to the relaxation-and-refilling-the-creative-well part of this trip," Jun added.

Dietyr kept the variety of witty comments he had to himself and stood, then stripped as fast as he could. Jun did the same. That was when Nirin did bolt, toward the bedrooms.

Dietyr was as fast as she was, but he had the table and Jun to navigate around. Jun had decent speed himself, but he wasn't a shifter. By the time the two of them turned down the hallway, the doors to all three bedrooms were closed and her scent led right up to every door. She was playing, and he loved it.

Jun looked up at him. "Split up, or check each room together?"

Dietyr hooked his hand around the back of Jun's neck and pulled him in for a kiss. Their lips crashed together with enthusiastic hunger. After a moment, Dietyr let them both up for air. "We all agree. Together is the way we're moving forward."

Jun's grin lit up the hallway.

They checked Dietyr's room first—it was closest to the main living area and the front entrance. She wasn't in there. Then they checked her room, at the other end of the hall and on the other side of Jun's. When they finally slid open the door to Jun's room, Dietyr wasn't particularly surprised. Jun's was the largest, with the best bed and the most interesting view. Not that any of them were going to be doing much water viewing in the immediate future.

Dietyr let Jun go in first. Just as Dietyr was entering, a shadow darted and almost got past him. But he managed to wrap an arm around its waist and turn his body so it would have to take him all the way down to the floor to make it farther. Then Jun was there, arms wrapped around the both of them, turning the moment into an embrace.

She relaxed in their arms, laughing softly. Dietyr couldn't remember the last time he'd heard her laugh freely.

This. They were good for one another.

"Caught you," he murmured.

"Mmm." She smiled. "Both of you. What will you do with me now?"

"Now" being the operative word. They weren't worrying about next steps anymore. Those could wait until the morning.

Jun pressed a kiss to the side of her neck, just below her ear. "Can you take both of us?"

She stilled, her heart rate speeding up. The scent of her arousal sharpened. She looked up at Dietyr, and he gave a slow, lazy grin. "We need words, love."

She licked her lips and nodded. "Yes."

CHAPTER 25

NIRIN HAD BEEN the one to start this game. They'd each been vulnerable, trying so hard to communicate clearly without pressuring one another. The tension had drawn taut inside her, and she'd had to break it somehow. Inviting them to play, to chase and catch her, did that—plus provided a way for her to manage the happiness and sheer nervous energy that burst as they had confirmed they'd planned to stay together. To give this new dynamic between the three of them a try.

Now, they'd caught her, and she couldn't help her wide grin or the way her nipples tightened in the cool air of the room. They were going to share her.

She felt suddenly shy as Dietyr loosened his hold on her and led her to the bed. Jun followed, holding her hand. Just as they reached the bed, Jun pulled her to him for a deep kiss. He took his time about it, coaxing her to open her mouth for him and tasting her. He coasted his hands up her arms, over her shoulders, and down to the small of her back. He hugged her close, then set his hands on her hips and gently pressed her backward until she sat in Dietyr's waiting lap.

Dietyr's hands were warm as they slipped around her waist and up to cup her breasts. Jun leaned over them both, resting his hands on Dietyr's knees as he shared an equally long kiss with Dietyr. She pressed little kisses along Jun's collarbone, reveling in the feeling of being caught in the circle of their embrace.

"I want to taste," Jun murmured. Then he was kneeling in front of her.

Dietyr shifted his legs under hers and parted his knees, spreading her legs with his. He reached with one hand to grip the inside of her thigh, and she groaned.

"I love your hands," she admitted, squirming in his hold, just a little bit.

Dietyr's erection was hot and hard against her ass. When he chuckled, she felt the rumble of it in his chest at her back.

Jun placed one of his hands on her opposite thigh, mirroring Dietyr's grip. She sucked in a breath and looked down at him. He gave her a terrible smirk, then licked her in a long stroke.

She shouted. Couldn't help it. She was already primed and incredibly sensitive. It was Jun's turn to chuckle. Then he proceeded to lick and kiss and suck until all she could do was let her head fall back against Dietyr's shoulder and clutch at anything she could hold on to. Which was mostly Dietyr's forearm.

Dietyr held her for Jun to feast, and Dietyr wasn't just watching. He trailed hot kisses along her neck and over her shoulder. He palmed one of her breasts and brushed the pad of his thumb over her taut nipple, teasing.

"So glad you didn't go," Dietyr muttered into her ear.

"Would've followed you this time. Couldn't let you leave again without at least trying."

She let her eyelids flutter shut at the sound of his voice almost cracked with emotion. Jun circled her clit with the tip of his tongue, then closed his mouth over her and sucked. Her orgasm hit and she shattered in ecstasy. The two of them held her as she was caught in the throes of her pleasure, Jun continuing to lick and suck gently, drawing it out while Dietyr murmured encouragements.

She had barely come back to herself when Dietyr coaxed her up and turned her to face him. He lay back on the bed and encouraged her to straddle him. Somewhere to the side, she heard Jun open the bedside drawer and retrieve necessities.

"I think our lady is ready," Dietyr said.

Jun pressed a kiss to her shoulder. "Think so?"

"You want to help?" Dietyr asked.

"Absolutely." Jun wrapped his hand around the base of Dietyr's cock, then pumped once, drawing a growl out of Dietyr. Then he sprayed a condom on Dietyr. "Are you ready to ride, love?"

On her knees, with hands braced on Dietyr's chest, she peered down between her thighs at Dietyr's erection. He was very ready and eager. Very.

"Ready." She breathed out the affirmative. They were all using words as best they could.

She eased back, letting Jun hold Dietyr steady for her. She wiggled just a bit, rubbing herself over the head of Dietyr's cock until he muttered a curse and fisted the sheets in his hands. Then she let his tip stretch her entrance. He was big for her, big enough that she had to take a long, slow breath as she lowered herself onto him.

"Fuck, you're so tight." Dietyr forced the words through a clenched jaw. "Are you okay?"

"Yes." She let the word draw out with her moan as the girth of him stretched her inner muscles. Finally, she had him to the hilt. She blew a loose lock of hair out of her eyes. "Wow."

Jun laughed. "I know, right?"

She couldn't help it—she laughed too.

Dietyr groaned. "I'm glad you both appreciate me, but if you keep laughing, I'm not going to last the way I want to."

"I'm not sorry." Nirin smiled and leaned forward to give him a kiss.

He didn't seem mad, the way he returned her kiss enthusiastically.

Behind her, Jun's hands smoothed over her ass and down the backs of her thighs. "This is a really tempting view."

Dietyr's arms slid up her back, and he spoke against her lips. "Ready for more?"

More. She was feeling so greedy. "Yes, please."

Dietyr flexed his hips, and the drag of his length inside her made her eyes roll up with pleasure. The spray of a condom let her know Jun was preparing. He caressed her hip to let her know he was behind her again. Cool fingertips spread lube around her anus, then pressed inside, preparing her.

"This isn't your first time this way, is it?" Jun asked.

She shook her head. "Not my first time with a single partner, but double penetration is new."

Dietyr pressed a kiss to her temple. "You sure you want this?"

"Yes, with you two, yes." She tightened her inner muscles to make her point, and Dietyr groaned.

"I'll go slow," Jun said. She felt the tip of his cock testing her. "Tell me if you need me to stop anytime."

"I will," she promised. "But, Jun, I want to feel you both."

It was Jun's turn to groan as he pressed carefully into her.

The stretch took her breath away. It was intense. Dietyr must have felt it too because he let out a huff. She smiled at Dietyr and nipped his collarbone. Jun continued to press into her, and Dietyr swallowed her moan with a kiss. Finally, she could feel Jun's hips flush against her backside, and she felt so incredibly full.

"Breathe." Jun sounded like he was reminding all of them.

And all of them did. They remained like that for several breaths, just feeling one another.

"Okay?" Jun asked.

"Good," Nirin whispered softly. "So, so good."

"Incredible," said Dietyr.

"I'm going to move now," Jun said. And he did.

He pulled out and pressed in just as slowly as the first time. As he did, Dietyr pulled his hips back. The two of them found a rhythm, and pleasure built low in her belly and up into her chest as she concentrated on breathing in and out with the waves of sensation. Every stroke drove her higher and higher, until she couldn't hold on to it all anymore and she crested into orgasm again with a shout.

Dietyr cursed, and his hips flexed upward as he came, then Jun pulled back and pushed in again one more time before he jerked against her and came too.

She was panting, blinking her eyes rapidly to clear her vision. Jun pulled out of her first, carefully. Then he helped her roll to one side of Dietyr. This time, Jun was the one to retrieve washcloths for all of them.

The three of them curled up in the bed, idly stroking one another's skin and nuzzling one another.

Dietyr stirred finally. "One more question."

"Hmm?" Nirin asked.

Finally, she didn't feel the need to tense, brace for impact, when he had that serious tone.

"Are we exclusive?"

Jun tensed next to her, and she pressed up on one elbow to look at them both, waiting for Jun's answer.

Jun looked from Dietyr to her. "I want to focus on what's between the three of us."

Dietyr nodded. "I'm not interested in anyone outside the two of you."

The two of them looked at her.

There'd been so many questions asked and answered between them all. This dynamic had already pressed her firmly outside her former comfort zones, and she didn't mind at all. It felt good to be with them. No nerves or desire to get away. These two felt right.

"Just us," she whispered. "I only want us."

"Good." Jun kissed each of them in turn. "Because I'm pretty sure I'm in love with you both."

The End

Thank you for reading *An Idol with Luv*. I've got more fun planned with these grumpy bodyguards and shiny intergalactic idols.

In the meantime, check out the original Triton Experiment series, starting with Hunting Kat.

I've got more shifter romances and contemporary fantasy planned soon. Be sure you never miss a new release announcement. Sign up for my newsletter!

ACKNOWLEDGMENTS

My deepest thanks to Uncle Gary and Uncle Greg for your love, encouragement, and willingness to answer any question.

Thank you to Wil, Alex, Kenna, Christina, Koren, Gabriel and Cooper for your early feedback as I was exploring these characters.

Thank you to Tara Rayers for your editorial expertise. Your insight and suggestions were on point, as always.

Love to Matthew for your support and encouragement.

Finally, thank you to my readers. I hope you've enjoyed this return to the Triton Experiment universe.

Piper J Drake is the author of Wings Once Cursed & Bound, book 1 of her fantasy romance Mythwoven series.

Piper is also the author of the bestselling romantic suspense series, the True Heroes, multiple series in paranormal romance and science fiction romance, as well as several standalone novels, short stories, and rpgs.

She is the cohost of the 20 Minute Delay podcast with Gail Carriger, a day job frequent flyer, gamer, foodie, and wanderer. Usually not lost.

Want the earliest updates, sneak peeks, and exclusive content from Piper? Sign up for her newsletter.